I Gave My Heart To A Jersey Killa

Tina J

Copyright 2019

__Warning:__

This book is strictly Urban Fiction and the story is **__NOT__**

__REAL__!

Characters will not behave the way you want them to; nor will they react to situations the way you think they should. Some of them may be drug addicts, kingpins, savages, thugs, rich, poor, ho's, sluts, haters, bitter ex-girlfriends or boyfriends, people from the past and the list can go on and on. That is what Urban Fiction mostly consists of. If this isn't anything you foresee yourself interested in, then do yourself a favor and don't read it because it's only going to piss you off. □□

Also, the book will not end the way you want so please be advised that the outcome will be based solely on my own thoughts and ideas. I hope you enjoy this book that y'all made me write. Thanks so much to my readers, supporters, publisher and fellow authors and authoress for the support. □□

Author Tina J

More books from me:

The Thug I Chose 1, 2 & 3

A Thin Line Between Me and My Thug 1 & 2

I Got Luv For My Shawty 1 & 2

Kharis and Caleb: A Different Kind of Love 1 & 2

Loving You Is A Battle 1 & 2 & 3

Violet and The Connect 1 & 2 & 3

You Complete Me

Love Will Lead You Back

This Thing Called Love

Are We In This Together 1,2 &3

Shawty Down To Ride For a Boss 1, 2 &3

When A Boss Falls in Love 1, 2 & 3

Let Me Be The One 1 & 2

We Got That Forever Love

Aint No Savage Like The One I Got 1&2

A Queen and A Hustla 1, 2 & 3

Thirsty For A Bad Boy 1&2

Hassan and Serena: An Unforgettable Love 1&2

Caught Up Loving A Beast 1, 2 & 3

A Street King And His Shawty 1 & 2

I Fell For The Wrong Bad Boy 1&2

I Wanna Love You 1 & 2

Addicted to Loving a Boss 1, 2, & 3

I Need That Gangsta Love 1&2

Creepin With The Plug 1 & 2

All Eyes On The Crown 1,2&3

When She's Bad, I'm Badder: Jiao and Dreek, A Crazy

Love Story 1,2&3

Still Luvin A Beast 1&2

Her Man, His Savage 1 & 2

Marco & Rakia: Not Your Ordinary, Hood Kinda Love 1,2

& 3

Feenin For A Real One 1, 2 & 3

A Kingpin's Dynasty 1, 2 & 3

What Kinda Love Is This: Captivating A Boss 1, 2 & 3

Frankie & Lexi: Luvin A Young Beast 1, 2 & 3

A Dope Boys Seduction 1, 2 & 3

My Brother's Keeper 1. 2 & 3

C'Yani & Meek: A Dangerous Hood Love 1, 2 & 3

When A Savage Falls for A Good Girl 1, 2 & 3

Eva & Deray 1 & 2

Blame It On His Gangsta Luv 1 & 2

Falling For The Wrong Hustla 1, 2 & 3

Haven *Reaper* Banks

"A'ight grams. Thanks for the food but I gotta go." I tossed the paper plate in the trash and threw the empty soda bottle in the recycling bin. My mom didn't play that. She's all about the environment with her corny ass.

Every Sunday she made us stop whatever we were doing and have brunch or dinner with her. It's always a comedy show over here between her, my pops and two uncles. It's never a dull moment. Today was dinner which I'm glad because it gave me something to do before I handle this other bullshit.

"Come here Haven." My grams whispered. I laughed because it meant she's about to ask me to do something sneaky for her ass. Grams is in her early seventies and not only does she smoke weed, but she has a man. You wouldn't know by looking at her because she looks good for her age.

"What's up?" I grabbed the paper towel after washing my hands.

"Where's my trees?" I reached in my pocket and handed her what she asked for.

"Don't tell your mother either. Sometimes she has the holy ghost and other times she's don't." My grams stayed talking shit.

"Ok damn."

"Boy don't let Christian hear you cursing." I peeked around the corner and he was in the room with his wife.

Christian is my brother, but we have different fathers. My mom met my pops at work and she already had a son. He helped my mother out of a bad situation, they got together, he adopted Christian and the rest is history. We don't consider ourselves half anything and from the records at city hall, my pops Wolf, is his father.

"I know right." Christian is the Deacon at the big ass Baptist church over on 22nd street. He has my bad ass nephew CJ and his wife can't stand me, which most women can't but who cares.

She's a bitch who only wants Christian for his money. He acts all pussy whipped because she's the one who broke his

8

virginity. I told his dumb ass to try new pussy before marrying her. He was so in love he couldn't see past her non taking dick ass. Hell no I ain't fuck her but a few times I crashed at their house and all she did is complain, complain, complain.

Talking about Christian you can't put it there or it hurts in that position. I ain't never heard such nonsense in my life. My father told him she's a dead lay if she doing all that. My mom won't get in it because she knows the bitch's mother. I told her FUCK THEM! They fake bougie anyway.

Now whenever he goes anywhere with me she wants him to keep her on the phone. I be hanging up on her dumb ass. My brother ain't about to be stressed when he's outside the house. Christian be mad too because she'll hold out on giving him sex. I told him to be happy because she can't fuck. He gets mad as hell.

"Whatever. I'm out."

"Be safe Haven." Grams tossed her hands in different directions in front of me.

"What you doing?"

9

"I don't know. I see the preacher doing it at church. I figured it keeps people outta harms way." I busted out laughing and told her she going to hell for mocking the pastor.

"See y'all later." I heard someone suck their teeth. I looked at Armonie who was trying her hardest to get to me but with the slight disability she wasn't fast enough.

"I can't wait until my brother gets some new pussy and leaves you standing there stuck on stupid."

"HAVEN!" My mom shouted.

"You know I don't like her and she always got something to say. Dumb bitch." I barked.

"Christian are you gonna let him speak to me in that manner?" His wife asked with her hands on her hips.

"Shut yo conceited ass up." My cousin Jax chimed in.

"A'ight Haven and Jax. That's enough." I heard Christian coming behind me.

"Teach your wife to respect royalty when she's in this house."

"Royalty?"

"Enough Elaina damn." We all stared at Christian because he never gets upset. Her mouth hit the floor.

"Are you ok?" My mom asked him.

"He's good ma. He just needs his dick sucked better and some decent pussy." Elaina was mad as fuck.

WHAP! I swung my body.

"You lucky I love your short ass otherwise I would've body slammed you." I told Armonie who smacked me on the back of my head.

"Bye y'all." My aunt Journey said folding her arms.

"You coming Christian?" I was being smart.

"I hope something bad happens to you." Elaina spat and all hell broke loose.

Armonie jumped on her and my aunt, mom or grams couldn't get her off. My uncle Colby had to come in with uncle Jax and my father to get her off. I damn sure wasn't breaking it up and neither were any of my other cousins. My aunt Venus couldn't stand her either, so she sat there with a smile on her face.

"What the fuck happened?" My uncle Colby barked. Armonie is his princess so if anyone messed with her, he flipped out.

"Christian I'm ready to go." Elaina got up off the floor wiping her clothes and tryna fix her hair. She had a swollen eye, bloody nose and some of her nails were broken.

"Go wait in the car."

"Christian!" She whined.

"NOW!" He barked and I smiled. We all watched her walk out the house. My nephew came downstairs unaware of anything that transpired which is good because regardless if I fucked with his mom or not, I wouldn't want him to see her get beat up.

"Look. I know y'all want what's best for me and I appreciate it but Armonie you can't beat on my wife."

"She asked for it Christian." He walked over and hugged her.

"I know she did. Y'all may think I'm not paying attention, but you're mistaken."

"Word?" Me and Jax asked at the same time.

12

"Yea. Come on son." He picked my nephew up and walked towards the door.

"I heard you loud and clear grams and you're right. I'm going to do it after this revival we have next week. Love y'all." He left and we switched and turned to my grandmother.

"What?" She played coy.

"Well?" My mom questioned.

"He's divorcing her." She told us and smiled.

"That's all I needed to hear." I bid my farewells and left with Colby Jr and Jax. I still had a mission to complete tonight.

Hold up. Let me rewind for everyone wondering. My name is Haven Banks Jr. and my father is the one and only Wolf from Tina J's book Ain't No Savage Like The One I Got. For those who may not know, he has a sister named Journey who married Colby. My pops also has a brother named Jax who married Colby's sister Venus. You don't have to read the book because this is our story and trust, it's way different from theirs. Now back to the story.

****

13

"You sure about this cuz? I know how much you were feeling her." Colby Jr. said putting on his vest. We weren't sure it was needed but we never went in a situation blinded or undressed. What I mean by undressed is without a vest, weapons and masks. In this situation I could care less who saw me.

"Positive. Y'all ready?" I took the last pull of the blunt and put it out.

"Yup." Him and Jax responded at the same time.

"Let's roll." We stepped out the car, glanced around the neighborhood and walked to the door.

Short story of why I'm here. My girl who I've been with for two years thought because I'm busy, she could fuck other niggas and I wouldn't find out. I think she forgot who I was or thought because it's a corny nigga she fucking I wouldn't find out.

If you're wondering we're at his house and not my girls. She ain't crazy enough to have the nigga at her place. Funny how I have the key tho. I chuckled to myself because people will give you anything when there's a gun inside their mouth.

14

His mother almost shit on herself when I came for the spare key. I knew she had one because after doing my research, she comes by a lot to clean his house.

Anyway, as I stepped in the house and noticed the clothes scattered all around, it angered me because Juicy is or should I say, was mine. Her real name is Anita but I call her Juicy since her ass is big, and her breasts sit up nice thanks to me. I paid for the transformation because she was having insecurities about her body or some shit. Also, her pussy stays wet and gushy which is another reason she had the name.

"Mmmm. You feel so good." Her voice boomed through the house making me cringe with thoughts of him touching her. I'm not no soft ass nigga but that's my bitch allowing another man to bring her to ecstasy.

"You sure cuz? I can do it for you." Jax stopped me at the steps.

"I'm good y'all." I reassured them. It's never a sight you wanna see but I'm good. I didn't have to search any rooms because the door to where they shared a bed was open. It hurt to see Juicy riding him and feeling herself the way she does me but again, I'ma be a'ight.

"I'm about to cum baby." She moaned out and just as her body began to shake and release her sweetness, I snatched that bitch off his dick by her hair.

"OH MY GOD!" I gripped it tighter and flung her on the floor.

"Who the hell are you?" This punk even spoke corny.

"Your worse fucking nightmare."

"Reaper I'm sorry." Juicy sat against the wall with her knees pressed to her chest.

"REAPER? There's only one man I know by that name and..." The man's eyes grew wide with fear.

"Anita you didn't tell me the Reaper was your man." I cocked my gun back.

"Oh so you knew she had a man?"

"Yea but she said he was neglecting her sexually and..." This dude was petrified so bad, he pissed himself.

"I was neglecting you sexually Juicy? I mean you wasn't fucking me once or twice a week?"

16

"Reaper please. Let me explain." She cried.

"No need for your emotional constipation. Dude here told me you weren't getting enough dick so you had to look elsewhere. Isn't that right? What's your name?"

"Purnell."

"Damn Juicy. You couldn't find someone with a hood name?" I shook my head. Colby and Jax waited at the door for my cue.

"Look. I'm sorry about this. I won't sleep with her ever again." Purnell pleaded.

"You're right about that."

POW! I shot him in the face and it exploded due to the hollow point bullets I had inside.

"AHHHHH!" Juicy screamed and covered her mouth.

"Your turn." I sat on the bed.

"Colby let me get that knife." He walked in on the phone. I took it out his hand and had Juicy come over to me. At first, she didn't move but when I barked, she ran over.

"Bitch, I wish you would try and sit on my lap with y'all nut coming out your dirty ass pussy. Sit on the got damn

17

floor." I pressed down on her shoulder and sat her in front of me.

"I gave you everything your heart desired and this how you do me?" I spoke in her ear to make sure she heard me.

"Reaper I'm sorry. I don't know why I cheated."

"Too late for regrets now." I tilted her head to look at me.

"They say breaking up with your first love will hurt the most." She started crying hysterically when I placed the knife under her neck.

"AHHHHHH. Reaper what are you doing?" She asked when I slid the knife under her breasts. It wasn't a deep cut yet because I wanted her to feel a little pain first.

"Before I kill you, I'm gonna take back those breast and ass implants I paid for." I started putting my black gloves on.

"What?" She tried to move away and I snatched her back.

"Yea. I paid a lotta money for these shits and I'm sure I can make money on the black market for them." Just as I said that, I wrapped my arms around her throat and sliced one of her breasts in half.

"AHHHHHH!" Her screams did nothing to me.

"Bring me some tape." Jax brought it in and the guys we paid to clean up our mess stepped in at the same time. I had my cousin tape her mouth.

I pushed her from in front of me and laid her on the ground. She tried kicking and screaming until I knocked her out with one punch. I sliced the other breast, dug inside and took the silicone out. I flipped her over and did the same to her ass cheeks. Not once did I worry about hurting her or the amount of pain she's in. She wasn't worried about inflicting any on me. Granted, it's different but she'll learn, won't she?

"Any of y'all want these?" I tossed them towards Colby, and he jumped back.

"You play too fucking much."

"A'ight. I think we're done here." I told them and took the gloves off.

"You know she's still breathing right?" Jax asked as we watched her taking slow breaths. Blood was pouring outta her body.

POW!

"Not no more. I need a drink?" I stepped over the bitch.

"This place needs to be up in flames in less than two minutes." I told the guys who were scared to death of me. They've seen me do some wild shit.

I walked out the door and not even 60 seconds later, the guys exited with two body bags. We backed our cars up and within thirty seconds, the house exploded.

That's right. I'm THE MOTHERFUCKING REAPER so when you see me coming, get the fuck out my way because nobody is exempt from my wrath.

Christian Banks

"My son will not return to that house." My wife Elaina all but yelled as I placed my son in the bath.

When we left my parents' house, the car ride was quiet, which I appreciated because I needed time to think. Think about why I stayed in a marriage that was dead before it started. I definitely loved Elaina but because she's the one who broke my virginity, I felt staying with her was the right thing to do. Not knowing what sex is supposed to be like because I stayed a virgin until the age of 22, I thought she was the best thing ever.

In the beginning, there wasn't anything she couldn't get from me. Money, sex, a car and eventually a house. You would think she appreciated it but after a couple years of marriage all she did is take, take, and take. She had a great job at the post office; yet she refused to use a dime of her money to purchase anything. It never bothered me until recently. The large purchases were unnecessary in my eyes; especially when she needed nothing.

I never thought I'd be filing for divorce or even thinking about it because Elaina was my everything at one time. Now all she does is nag, complain and make threats on my brother. It's her fault they don't get along and no I don't get involved when they argue because she starts it. When it gets too bad, then I'll say something otherwise, I let her handle the mess she creates.

"My son will be there and stop wishing bad luck on my brother." I told her as I washed CJ up. Usually I'd allow him to stay in longer but I see this argument escalating.

"No he won't. That man disrespects me any chance he gets, and you say nothing. Then, your cousin jumped on me and had it not been for your father and uncles no one was gonna break it up." I lifted lil Christian out the bath after rinsing the soap off and went in his bedroom.

"Elaina, you spark up the argument every time. What is it about Haven you don't like? Huh? Is it the fact he doesn't bite his tongue or the fact he doesn't appreciate the way he sees you treat his brother?" She sucked her teeth and stormed out my sons' room. She knew just like I did those are the real reasons.

Haven is just like my pops and won't allow anyone to harass or aggravate his loved ones. Elaina has done both over the last two years and all of my family are tired of seeing it. Today got bad because she wished back luck on him and my cousin beat her ass.

Me, Haven and Armonie are the closest out of the grandkids. Jax and Colby are close and then the younger kids have their own connections. Its just how we grew up. She doesn't understand why and it's probably because she's the only kid. It doesn't help that her mom is fake and phony. I think it rubbed off on my wife because she's just as bad now.

"I don't wanna fight Elaina. I'm tired and wanna make love to my wife; that's all." Ugh yea, I'm going to keep having sex with her until we divorce.

"Not tonight Christian." I stopped taking off my pants and looked at her.

"Why is that?"

"Because my face is messed up and I don't feel like sucking your dick." Now her eyes rolled in her head.

"Fine." I didn't argue, fuss or fight. I know how to get myself off and I'm not about to beg for it. I stepped in the bathroom, handled my need, showered and went to sleep in the room with my son. If I ain't getting none, there's no need to be in the same bed.

"Why are you in here?" She opened the door after I closed it.

"My wife doesn't wanna be with me sexually and claims her face is messed up, so why am I setting myself up to get aggravated?"

"Is this marriage only about sex? I mean how come you can't hold me and say it'll be alright." I fixed the pillow the way I wanted.

"Because these days, nothing I do or say will accommodate your needs. Can you close the door on your way out?" She huffed and slammed the door on the way out. *Spoiled bitch.*

****

"Thank you for coming." I shook hands with some older women who visited from another church during revival week. Today was the last day and I couldn't wait for it to be over. A long week of services is a lot when you're going through things at home with your wife.

"Anytime Deacon Banks. I'm sorry Mrs. Banks couldn't make it to the services."

"Thanks, and I'll let her know her presence was missed." Her and the other ladies with her walked out.

"You deserve better than Elaina." Stormy whispered in my ear.

"That's what they say but here I am about to file for a divorce. I know it's going to be a spectacle within the pews." I spoke about the gossiping within the congregation. We both busted out laughing and I couldn't help but stare at how beautiful she is.

She was tall, maybe 5'6 with light brown eyes. She wasn't thick or petite, but she did have quite a bit of curves. Her appearance has never been short of gorgeous and the two of us grew up in church. We've become the best of friends and even though she's always been pretty, and for some reason I'm just noticing. Maybe it's because my focus was becoming a deacon and then Elaina came in my life. Who knows but whatever the case, she really is a great friend to me.

You may not remember but her parents are Hassan and Serena Burns from one of Tina J's older series. He's the pastor of the church and his following is huge. My mom used to bring us here all the time as kids. Haven went in a totally different direction, where I felt church was my calling.

"Where is the old bat?" Stormy glanced around the church. I shrugged my shoulders and left her standing there.

"You ok Deacon Banks?" Pastor Burns asked when I passed his office.

"I'm good. Just thinking about what we discussed last week. I think it's time." He nodded.

"You can use my lawyer if you need." I thanked him and walked down to my office. It wasn't big; yet it was comfortable and peaceful.

"How you just leave me standing there? Rude." Stormy said closing the door. She laid on the couch and flipped the TV on like always. I moved her legs out the way and sat next to her.

"You think I'm a good husband?" She muted the TV and looked at me.

"I can't answer that Christian, but you are a great Deacon, an amazing father and even better friend. Don't let her make you feel less of a man because things between you two didn't work out. It may not be meant for you to be together. Hell, I don't think there's any man out there who can handle her." I chuckled a little and rested my elbows on my knees. She used her hand to make my face meet hers.

"Christian there are other great women out there who would love a man like you. I think you should keep Haven, Jax and Colby away from her tho." We both laughed.

"I don't mind being alone, I mean it's how I've been for a while in the house anyway. I just don't know how to date a woman. Stormy she's all I know." She stood in front of me and reached her hands out. Mine connected with hers and we were now staring each other down.

"You know more than you think Christian." She placed her hand on the side of my face and I put mine on hers. Just as I went to lean in for a kiss there was a knock on the door.

"I'm sorry Stormy. I shouldn't have done that or almost done that." She sat on the couch and picked her phone up.

"Why was the door shut?" Elaina spoke when I opened it up.

"You could've walked in so don't come in here making a scene over nothing." She stared at Stormy.

"I'm gonna go Deacon. We'll finish that conversation another time." She looked my wife up and down and laughed.

"Is something funny?" Stormy turned.

"Actually, it is. You see, we've had revival here all week and not once did you check in on your husband. Tonight, you roll up in here dressed like you're going out. Is it that hard to support your husband or are you too busy shopping?"

"Whatever I do with my husband is none of your concern." Stormy smiled.

"You're absolutely right but if I were you, I'd be careful about leaving him alone too long. There are way too

28

many women looking for a Deacon these days." She sashayed away and all I could think of was, is Stormy trying to tell me something? Nah, she has a man.

I closed the door again to make what I said earlier believable about her opening it if she wanted to. I'm glad she didn't because it would've been a mess.

"Are you fucking her?" Elaina questioned me as I went to take a seat at my desk.

"No and tell me why you find it appropriate to curse in a church?" I curse myself here and there but never in the house of God.

"Whatever. I wanna have sex but only in the missionary position. You're too big and I don't feel like hurting when I walk." She locked the door and started taking her clothes off.

"As appealing as it sounds, I'm gonna decline." I stopped her from removing her skirt.

"What?"

"I got work to do and if I feel like it when I get home, we can." I leaned back in my chair and waited to see the tantrum she'd throw.

"This is ridiculous. I can't even fuck my own husband. What good are you if I can't? Maybe I should go be another man."

"Make sure he has a small penis." I said in a non chalant way.

"Excuse me!"

"It seems mine is too big and since you never took the time out to get used to it, why not find someone smaller? You won't hurt or walk funny as you say and it won't crowd your throat. We all know you hate going down on me so be my guest to look elsewhere."

"Are you telling me to have an affair?" I grabbed my things because this isn't going anywhere, and I won't get any work done.

"I'm telling you it's over. I'm filing for divorce in the morning. Expect the papers in the mail." I opened the door for her to leave.

"If you go through with a divorce, I'll go to the cops about the extracurricular activities your brother is in." I yoked her up by the shirt, never dropping the things in my other hand. She doesn't know anything Haven does but I don't need her going down to the precinct tryna make them build a case on him either.

"Just because I'm not in the streets don't mean shit. Stop letting my Deacon status fool you. Take your ass to the cops with your lies and you'll see a side of me you never wanted to. Fuck with me if you want." I heard someone clear their throat and pushed her away from me.

"Everything good Deacon?" Pastor Burns asked and turned his face up at Elaina. No one and I mean no one cared for her.

"We good wife?" She sat on the ground with terror in her eyes.

"I can't hear you."

"Yes." She whispered but we heard her.

"Good. Serena wants you and lil man to stop by for dinner one day this week." I glanced over at Elaina on the floor.

"We'll be there." He patted me on the shoulder and escorted me to my car.

"I don't know what happened but I trust you had her yoked up for a reason." He said at the car. I explained what happened and he told me to start having her watched. Women like her don't go away easy.

"Oh Deacon." I was about to sit in my truck.

"What's up?"

"You and Stormy are both attached right now. Do not get anything started until it's finished."

"Stormy and I are only friends." He smirked.

"For now. Have a good night." He waved goodbye. I sat in my car smiling. Stormy is my friend and I'm keeping it that way. *I think.*

Vernon *VJ* Davis

"You're telling me you don't have the rent money?" I asked the chick Lily who stayed in the condos I owned.

Me and my sister Vanity had four different ones and we ran each of them with an iron fist. Meaning; there was no loud partying, niggas hanging out all night and if you BBQ'd just make sure you cleaned up. People from all ages and walks of life stayed in our condos and it's only right for everybody to respect one another's space. I've driven around areas where condos, townhomes and even houses look like shit and we not having that.

"Mr. Davis, I'm sorry. I lost my job and..." I put my hand up because she was blowing my high. My boy Mycah and I smoked two blunts outside my office and finished right before she stepped in.

"When did you stop working?" I leaned back in my chair staring. I just saw her there last week.

The chick in front of me was beautiful. Her body was bad, and her baby daddy recently got locked up for drugs. He was a big-time hustler out here and she's a stripper. What I couldn't understand is how she had no money. Did it disappear?

"Where's the money your man left behind?" She shrugged her shoulders. I'm not stupid. Either she spent it or tryna save it. Whatever the case, if she ain't got the money, she's outta here.

"Look, today's the 2nd and you have until the 5th to come up with the rent." I watched her pretend to be upset.

"Where am I gonna come up with that kinda money? $1750 is a lot." I rose outta my seat and headed to the door.

"Let me school you real quick shorty in case your mama never did." I opened the door and gestured for my sister to come in. I always had her around in case a bitch got stupid

"Never let a man talk you into renting or buying something you can't afford if he walks away or in your case, goes to jail." She went to speak and I held my hand up

"He knew you had his child and still left you to fend for yourself." She nodded and I still didn't believe her.

"A word of caution." She wiped those fake ass tears falling down her face.

"You're a stripper and a good one I might add." She smirked. Of course I've seen her in action and she can fuck a pole up.

"There's no reason why you rocking that Birkin bag, Giuseppe heels, all those diamonds and don't have the rent." She sucked her teeth.

"I recommend you sell that shit and be here with the money on the 5th or you, yo kid, all your furniture and clothes will be out by the time you make him lunch." She walked to the door.

"If you know how bad I am on the pole, let me do some things on yours." She ran her hand down my chest and I gripped her wrists before pushing her away. I could see my sister shaking her head.

"Your best friend is my fucking girl and has been for years. How you think she'd feel knowing you tryna fuck?"

"She shouldn't feel anything; especially, when her dumb ass brags about the things you do in the bedroom." She twirled her tongue and I shook my head.

"And she'll be the only one who'll know what's it's like. Bye." She rolled her eyes.

"I know you tired of the same pussy." This bitch is really pushing it.

"Bitch move the fuck on." My sister mushed her in the head and slammed the door in her face. That's exactly why I kept her around. My sister isn't a bully and she doesn't get in any bullshit but when her siblings needed her, she's right there and we do the same for her.

"What the hell is wrong with her?"

"What can I say? Mecca ran her damn mouth and now her friends wanna ride this ride." She threw the pen at me and went into her office. I followed and leaned on the side of her door.

"Anyway, Antoine is coming for the week so I may be here, and I may not." She spoke of her boyfriend out in Jersey.

36

They've been messing around for almost a year now and I think they both strung the fuck out. He visits every other weekend and niggas around knew not to fuck with her. He's a thorough ass dude and his name rang bells in the streets even though he wasn't from here. I didn't know him until they got together but then again, I've never sold a drug in my life or went to jail. I'm a legit ass businessman and I don't plan on changing shit. They're funny as hell together and I actually like him for her.

Vanity went out there quite a bit to help my uncle with their condos out there. None of his kids wanted to be in the business and he knew not to ask me. It's not that I didn't like Jersey. Shit, I was born and raised there up until I was thirteen when my parents decided to move down here to Virginia and open up condos. They had some in Maryland too and my sister loved to travel so it was a no brainer for her.

"Word? Tell the nigga to hit me up."

"Hell no! The last time he came, you had him so fucked up he could barely move for two days." I laughed because we went to the strip club and got so fucked up, she had to come get us.

"Whatever. I'll hit him up myself."

"VJ, let me be around him for the first two days, damn. It's been a couple weeks and I need some dick."

"Bye Vanity." I moved away from her door.

"Oh, but I can hear you say that trifling ho you fucking can suck you off." I busted out laughing. She couldn't stand Mecca and the feeling is mutual. However; my girl knew not to ever come out her face at my sister.

"Whatever. You cooking when he come?" She gave me the *duh* look.

"A'ight. I'll be over and we'll wait two days so you can have your moment." She flipped me the finger and I dipped off in my office.

****

"Pops, can you feel on mom later? I don't wanna see that shit." I had my face turned up at them. He called me over to talk.

"Be quiet VJ and where is Mecca?" My mom asked.

38

"Home I guess." I grabbed a banana out the fruit bowl.

"When y'all gonna move in together and have kids?" She asked and I almost choked.

"VJ you been together for a few years." She stood in front of me. My mom wanted grandkids bad as hell and being me and Vanity the only ones in real relationships, she was stressing us the fuck out over it.

"And I'm still not sure she the one." My father smirked. He and I spoke a lot about Mecca, and he told me she may not be the one. If I wanted to find my soulmate as he says, then she had to be put on the backburner because no woman is gonna play second while I try and find the right one.

"I want you to come with us to Jersey next weekend." My father said and walked in the other room.

"For?" I questioned because they go without me all the time.

"You mother wants to see Isa and you never go."

"I guess. It'll give me a break from Mecca."

"Bring her VJ. She has family there too." My mother chimed in coming down the stairs.

39

"Ma, she up under me enough."

"That's because she loves you." She kissed my cheek and left me and my father standing there.

"Your mother think she slick." I tossed the peel in the trash.

"What you mean?"

"She wants to move back up there." He said and smiled at her.

"And you're gonna go?" I asked and already knew the answer.

"Hell yea. My wife ain't going nowhere without me."

"Strung out ass. I'm out." I walked towards the door.

"When you meet the woman to string your ass out, I'm gonna pay her 20k." I started laughing.

"Why does every father say that to their son? Not every woman in the world who has a man can string them out." I was dead serious.

"Shittttt. All I'm gonna say is, when you meet her, you'll know."

"Whatever."

40

"I'm serious. You keep saying no chick will have you like me." He stood behind my mother and kissed her neck.

"A'ight bet pops. What happens if she never comes around?"

"Then I'll give you the money." I nodded and told him I'll see them in a few days.

I drove to my house and Mecca was sitting outside. I parked and stared at her get out. I loved her without a doubt but being in love hasn't happened for me yet. That strung out, can't eat, sleep or focus type of love ain't popping over here.

"Hey babe." She opened the car door for me. I stepped out and walked up my porch.

"Do you really have to throw Lily out? You know her son is my god baby and..." I shushed her. If she only knew the bitch tried to fuck me, I doubt she'd be going this hard for her.

"Business is business Mecca." I closed the front door and locked it.

"I told you not to send your friends to live in my buildings for this reason right here." She pouted.

"What you doing here anyway? I thought you had to work."

"I called out." I stopped going up the steps and turned to her.

"Why?"

"We haven't had sex in a week and I'm horny." I laughed because she can't even take the dick half the time.

Don't get me wrong, her pussy gets wet and all but the only thing I like for her to do is suck my dick. She's a pro at it and I can go to sleep afterwards. Maybe it's the reason I'm not in love. She doesn't offer the full package and a nigga wants it all.

"You better not ask me to stop."

"Whatever. Sometimes it hurts but don't play me. You love this pussy." I rolled my eyes since she was still walking behind me to the room.

"Just strip and meet me in the bathroom." She smiled and damn near ran in there. Let me grab my condoms because ain't no babies going in her.

Armonie Foster

"We'll be done in a few minutes." I told my cousin Haven when he stepped in the house. We were all going out tonight and since it's his club, it made sense for us to go with him.

"Hurry yo ass up." He sat on the couch and sparked up a blunt. I walked up the steps and checked on my best friend Ariel. She and I went to elementary school together and been friends ever since

"Ok bitchhhhhh. You look nice." She had on an all black romper showing off her tattoos. She loved getting them where I only had a few because they hurt. The shoes were all black Giuseppe's and her diamond necklace, earrings and bracelet kicked the entire outfit off. She had a short pixie style haircut and her face was beat like always.

"Can you get dressed? It's already after ten and who feels like dealing with all the ignorant ass men we walk by?" She complained.

"Alright." I stepped outta her room and in mine. I put my all black leather catsuit on along with the Louboutin heels. I also had diamonds to show off as well.

"Ok heffa. Don't let Freddy see you." I waved her off.

Freddy is my on and off again boyfriend. We've been together for two years and I have yet to give him my virginity. At first, I thought he was the one and couldn't wait to become a woman but after finding out he cheated, I broke up with him. I know men had needs but if you really loved a woman like you say, then waiting shouldn't have been an issue. Mind you after we broke up, I heard about him in the streets with other women.

However; he found his way home and I took him back because I really did love him. That was six months ago, and we have yet to indulge in any sexual activity. I won't even allow him to go down on me. If I did, it would only entice the situation and right now I need to focus on me. The type of relationship we have is perfect at times and not so much at others.

"Do I look even?" I asked Ariel because I have a slight disability. I have what's called a limb length discrepancy. It means one of my legs is shorter than the other. You can only tell if I'm not wearing shoes because it causes a slight limp. I was a premature baby and the doctor said it's a possibility it could've come from that or it's just nature. I'm not ashamed of it and no one bothers me about it.

I asked Ariel because when we go out, I do become self-conscious due to the number of gorgeous women in the club. Their bodies are brought, and they put us natural women to shame every time. We can sit in a club and say we don't hate but in our heads, we talking all types of shit about how fake they look and how their ass looks disgusting.

"You look fine sis." She stood behind me and stared in the mirror.

"We about to tear the club down." I told her and grabbed my clutch and phone.

"About damn time." Haven barked never turning around. As usual he was still smoking.

45

"Be quiet. You always got something to say." Ariel popped him on the back of his head. He swung his body around on the couch.

"Where the fuck you going in that outfit?" He asked me and stared at Ariel's clothes.

"Haven it's fine and Ariel has on something similar."

"That's what ho's wear but you're not a ho." Ariel stood in front of him.

"I ain't no ho." He looked her up and down.

"My bad. That's what dick sucking ho's wear." He shrugged his shoulders and she pushed him in the chest.

"For your information, I've only gone down on two guys." She had her hands on her hips.

"Not what the streets saying, and you know they talk." He gave her the side eye. Haven loved fucking with Ariel and she fell victim every time.

"I don't care what they say. I know how many times I've done it." She snatched her things up.

"I heard your head game needs some work." Her mouth dropped.

46

"Don't look at me." He put his hands up.

"If you want me to change the streets perception, feel free to work them jaws over here." He pointed to himself. I just shook my head.

"I would never." She stormed over to the door.

"I'm sure you had this same conversation with them." She rolled her eyes.

"You sure you don't want to? We got some time. Matter of fact, Armonie go upstairs real quick and let me fill her mouth up. I'll call you down soon as I nut." Ariel walked out the house. I don't know why she's mad. She should've just ignored him.

"Haven leave her alone. She gets enough shit from people off the street."

"Why? Is that where she performs at?"

"Ughhhh. You're so aggravating." We walked out the house and to the truck. Ariel stood there pouting. Haven laughed it off and unlocked the doors.

"We still got time Ariel." He joked and she stared out the window. I wasn't about to get into their petty argument because they'll be right back to speaking tomorrow.

****

"Packed as usual." I said stepping out the truck.

"I have you and the dick sucker in VIP." Ariel flipped him the bird. We followed behind him to the door and stepped away as security removed the red rope.

The song *Money* boomed through the speakers as we made our way to VIP. Each area was sectioned off by a small wall for privacy. You were only able to see in those sections if you walked past and even then it may be hard being they had sliding doors in front of them with curtains. Haven did the most with his club but the way him and Anita used to fuck, I'm not surprised. Too bad she's not gonna join us anymore. Haven didn't tell us she was dead, well I guess he did in his own way by saying the *Reaper* got her. Oh well, she knew like the whole world not to fuck him over, but I guess she thought as his woman she'd be exempt.

"A'ight. Bottle service will be here in a minute and the red button is right there." He pointed to it behind us. Its only for emergencies and it unlocked the sliding doors if they were closed. When you walk up the steps to get here you see signs that say press in case of emergencies. I know I appreciated it. One thing Haven didn't play, is rape and he refused to allow any woman to be uncomfortable and unable to leave.

"Remember Ariel. No sucking dick in front of my cousin. She needs to stay pure forever." He winked at me and she threw some ice from the bucket at him.

All my male cousins are over protective of the girls in the family but since I'm the first one, they're extra with me. Sometimes I love it and other times it gets on my nerves.

"OH MY GOD!" I saw Ariel staring down at her screen.

"WHAT?" She had me nervous.

"VJ is in town and over my parents." I smiled because he's her favorite cousin.

"Really? I haven't seen him in years." The last time I seen him we were twelve or thirteen. Their fathers owned apartment complexes and condominiums. They moved to Virginia to open up more spots and never returned. They come visit but he usually stays behind to handle the business.

"I know right. He FaceTime's me once in a blue moon but it's not the same as being around."

"Awww look at you about to cry."

"I am. Let me tell him where we are. Maybe he'll come by." I told her ok and put the order in for bottle service.

For the next two hours she and I drank and danced our ass off. It felt good to be free and not have any worries.

Both of us went to the bathroom and like I said, women were in there half naked with built up bodies. Ariel and I joked all the way to our VIP area and stopped when we noticed some dude kissing a chick in our section. I almost got turned on by how erotic the shit looked. It's like he was making love to her mouth.

"EXCUSE YOU! YOU'RE IN OUR SECTION!" I shouted over the music. The dude stopped, wiped his bottom lip and looked up.

"OH MY GOD! VERNONNNNNNN!" Ariel ran over and jumped in his arms. The chick didn't seem happy at all.

"Damn cuz. I miss you too." He hugged her tight and put her down giving me a better look.

Even when we were younger VJ was fine but got damn, he had my panties wet just by staring at him. His thug appearance and swag were ridiculous and had my ass not been a virgin I'd probably ask him to follow me in the bathroom. That's how sexy he looked.

"How did you know which section I was in?"

"Ugh, you told me in the text." Ariel smacked herself on the forehead and laughed because she forgot.

"This is Mecca. Mecca, this is my cousin Ariel." The way her face turned up had me and my friend on guard. Why the fuck she mad and we just met?

"Hi." She barely spoke and gave a fake wave.

"Whatever. VJ you remember Armonie right?" He looked past her and surveyed my entire body before making eye contact.

"Don't play me VJ." He moved towards me.

51

"Never that." He hugged me tight and his cologne invaded the hell outta my nostrils. Not only did he look good, he smelled it.

"You still sexy as fuck. It makes me wish I didn't bring her." He whispered in my ear and kissed my cheek. I swear, I wanted to open my mouth and get the same kiss he gave the Mecca bitch.

"Too bad for you." I flirted. His tongue slid over that bottom lip and my pussy began to thump. Never in my life has a man gotten me this hot and bothered; not even Freddy.

"Yea, it's too bad." He winked and walked over to where his chick stood.

"Now who about to be the dicksucking ho?" Ariel joked.

"If I knew how to, you got damn right. As sexy as he is, I'd suck the skin right off." She spit her drink out. I thought it was from laughing until I turned around and saw Freddy standing there.

"Let's go." He barked and gripped my arm. I would ask how he knew which section I was in, but everyone knew he was my man; including security.

"Go where?" I questioned because the liquor reeked through his clothes. If I didn't know any better, I'd say he spilled an entire bottle on himself.

"Outside to talk."

"No thanks." I tried to walk off and he gripped my arm tighter. Here we go with this shit.

VJ

"Why your cousin jump on you like that?" Mecca asked.

"Because we haven't physically seen one another in years. Why the fuck does it matter? You know we're related." I stood up.

"What about the other bitch. I saw how she looked at you." I smirked thinking about Monie. I've known her for as long as Ariel has but we weren't around one another a lot. She had her friends and I had mine. It didn't stop me from admiring her beauty back then and now. She's still one of the most beautiful women I've ever seen, and I've seen a lot.

She had a caramel complexion with a small mole above her right eye. She used to wear braces and now her teeth are perfect and white. Her petite and thick frame makes a nigga wanna keep her hidden from the world. I've never had a crush on her or even tried to get at her because even though we're a year apart, she was still too young for me. I wanted an older woman. Someone mature, had her head on straight and her own place.

At the age of 15, all of us young niggas were fucking cougars. It was all fun and games until they wanted a relationship and control. I had to tell one older bitch I already had a mother. Another one wanted me to discipline her ten-year-old kid. Bitch, I'm only eighteen how that look? I could tell you some stories about older women.

Anyway, when the nigga snatched her up, I glanced around the club to see if her peoples were here. I may not live in this area but their names held weight. They were feared by many; especially having someone named the Reaper in your family. The gruesome stories I heard about him, one would think he has the mind of a serial killer with the shit he does.

"You stay worried about other bitches when I'm here with you." I didn't mean to call Monie a bitch. I was just tryna make a point.

"Stay right here." I pointed to the chair.

"Where you going?"

"To piss damn. You wanna hold my dick for me while I do it?" What started out as a good night is ending up being annoying as usual.

Mecca and I have been together for a few years. She's from Virginia and had some family members up here too. I wish she go visit they ass; instead she sitting up under me.

She too is gorgeous and like I said before, her head skills are good but the pussy is just average. I've had better and if she didn't beg me to come, I wouldn't have brought her. My mother is the one who asked me to let her tag along.

My uncle Birch who is Ariel's father, and my pops brother wanted to open up more buildings in other parts of Jersey. He can do it on his own but I honestly think he wants his brother close. Shit, my mother Maylan and aunt Isa talk all day long, so I know they want to be close to each other again.

When we got to their house the two of them hugged for at least ten minutes. My pops and uncle Birch left them standing there and went out to smoke. I wanted to see my cousins too but damn.

"Tha fuck you doing in that nigga face?" I heard in the foyer area of the bathroom. No one was there when I came in. I turned the water on to wash my hands and grabbed some paper towels.

"Freddy, he's Ariel's cousin. Why you so insecure?"

"Ain't nobody insecure. Bitch, you better not be giving out no pussy." I shook my head. Niggas really be in their feelings when their woman speaks to someone else.

"I'm not, let go." Once she said that I rushed to open the door. My mom was a victim of domestic violence and almost died if my father didn't save her.

I don't play that shit so when I seen the dude with her hair wrapped around his hand and the busted lip, I tried to diffuse the situation. I don't know dude and my niggas ain't here, so I wasn't tryna get in no shit.

"Bro, you need to let her go." I saw Monie's eyes grow wide. She's probably embarrassed.

"Mind yo fucking business. This me and my bitch shit." He looked me up and down.

"Bitch?" I was mad as hell he called her that.

57

"I'm not gonna tell you again."

"VJ, I'm ok." I noticed the tears falling down her eyes.

"Yea VJ. Beat it."

"Not until you let her go." I was trying my hardest to remain calm.

"Fine." He swung her across the room and her head hit the wall knocking her out. I started beating this nigga ass. I zoned out thinking about my moms attacker and had no one pulled me off, I probably would've killed him.

"Call an ambulance." Somebody yelled after seeing his dumb ass knocked the fuck out. This is why I tried not to ever get angry. I get that supernatural strength and can't control myself.

"Monie, get up." I smacked her face a little.

"Grab me a wet paper towel." Someone passed me one and after rubbing it on her face a few times, she opened her eyes.

"You ok?" I asked.

"What happened?" She was still very confused.

"He threw you against the wall and you hit your head." I lifted her hair up to see how bad the gash was.

"Tha fuck going on in here?" I heard someone bark and everyone in the room dispersed.

CLICK! I felt the steel against my head.

"Who the fuck are you and why my cousin on the floor bleeding from the head and mouth?" The dude barked.

"Haven I'm fine. I must've been drunk and fell against the wall. He was helping me." My anger turned into disappointment. Disappointed she saved the nigga after he threw her against the wall like a rag doll.

"I don't want no problems." I put my hands up and stood.

"Thanks Vernon." She had pleading eyes for me not to mention what took place.

"Why the hell this nigga on the floor?" He put his gun up and when the EMT's showed up, he had them take her first. I left the scene and went to grab Mecca and my cousin. Ariel was dancing with a bottle in her hand and Mecca had an annoyed look as usual.

"Where's Monie?" Ariel questioned as if I would know. I did but my cousin didn't know that.

"We're leaving. You coming?" I asked ignoring her question.

"Let me get Armonie." I grabbed her arm.

"How long he been beating on her?" She blew her breath and I could see how watery her eyes got.

"I tried to help down there but she took up for him." I explained a little of what went down.

"She always does." She put her head down.

"Promise me you'll never allow a man to do that to you and if he did, you'll tell me or your brother."

"VJ, I know all about aunty Maylan. I'd never wanna go through the same thing."

"Why is she letting him do it?"

"She's scared and sadly he has mind control over her. No matter how many times I tell her it's not worth it, he'll come over with flowers, gifts and apologies." I shook my head and went to leave. Now she grabbed my arm and hugged me.

"He threatened to kill her if she left him." She whispered in my ear.

"We'll talk." I told her and walked down the steps with Mecca behind me.

"What's going on over there?" Mecca pointed to the bathroom area. Security was deep and you couldn't see pass the human wall they made.

"Probably some stripper being nasty or something." I wasn't gonna tell her Monie's business. They don't know one another and it's best to keep it that way.

****

"Mmmmm. VJ you feel good." I pulled outta Mecca and made sure both condoms were still intact. Its a nuisance using two, but I trusted no one.

"Turn over." I waited for her ass to toot in the air and inserted myself back in.

"Fuckkkkk. I'm gonna cum again." She gripped the sheets and threw her ass back. I wasn't really into the sex and wished she hurry up.

"Then cum on this dick." I smacked her ass and waited for her to get done. I was ready to nut but I never finished before a chick.

Once she released herself, I pulled out, took the condoms off and let her swallow my kids. In all the years I've had sex, a chick can never tell you I came inside her even in a condom. My ass was too scared to have kids and catch diseases.

I went in the bathroom, took a shower and headed out. I had things to do today and my first stop is to my cousin's house. I wanted to see her and check up on Monie. I haven't seen or heard from Ariel since it happened two nights ago.

I parked in front of their house and called my cousins phone. She opened the door and pointed to Monie's room. She stayed downstairs because of all the homework. She had a little longer to go in school and my cousin will be the first RN in the family. All the crazy things she's around, I'm sure it'll come in handy.

KNOCK! KNOCK! I didn't hear anything and opened the door. Monie was laying in her bed watching TV. I moved closer and noticed the busted lip was no longer there and she had a small patch on her forehead.

"What you doing here?"

"Is that anyway to speak to the man who saved your life?" She sat up.

"About that." I cut her off.

"No need for explanations and I'm not judging. I do think you should see someone because what he's doing is coward shit. Ain't no man gonna put his hands on a woman because she in a club." Her head fell back on the headboard.

"Thanks."

"No need." I sat closer, turned her face from side to side and examined it. Besides the bandage on her head she looked fine.

"Your owner know you here?" I chuckled at her being petty.

"I don't have an owner and never concern yourself with irrelevant people."

"Your girlfriend is relevant." Monie folded her arms across her chest.

"If you say so." I stared at this woman in front of me and could see how broken she was without saying a word. I don't know what my mom went through but it broke my father when he found her dying. She has to live with permanent scars and dentures and that's just the physical part. Mentally she's still messed up and has nightmares. I can't imagine what she's going through but I'm sure its similar.

"A'ight. I just wanted to check on you." I leaned over to kiss her cheek and she turned her head. Our lips connected and instead of us separating, we continued. My hand went behind her neck to bring her closer as if we weren't close enough.

"Oh my God VJ. I'm so sorry for kissing you." She pushed me away.

"It's all good Monie. We both wanted it."

"Really?"

"Yup." I leaned in to kiss her again and this time she somehow found her way in my lap. I squeezed her ass and the soft moan escaping her lips had my dick waking up.

"Ssss." I kissed her neck and caressed her breasts at the same time.

"You like this Monie?" My hands were in her shorts rubbing on her drenched pussy.

"Yesssss." She moaned. Her head was back as she began to ride the wave I felt coming. Her clit was extremely hard.

"Armonie, your mom is on the... oh shit." Ariel closed the door and Monie hopped off.

"I'm sorry." She pulled the covers up.

"Don't be." I stared in her eyes and caught myself from leaning in to kiss her again.

"It'll be our secret." I adjusted myself and kissed her forehead before leaving the room. I walked down the steps and Ariel sat on the couch smirking.

"Let me find out you busted her cherry." I stopped and looked at my cousin. Did she just say what I think she said?

"She's a virgin?" I asked to make sure.

"Got dammit. I thought y'all did it or she told you that's why Freddy bugging. He doesn't want anyone to be her first but him." I smirked. A virgin. Shit, I never been with one.

"Nah. I'm glad you told me tho. I would've had a hard time getting in." She tossed a pillow at me.

"You make me sick. Don't tell her I told you."

"I would've figured it out." I shrugged my shoulders.

"Boy please. Freddy has been around for two years and he hasn't even tasted her pussy. If you plan on getting some, I suggest you stick around for a few years."

"I'm not him and my swag on point." We both laughed.

"I wouldn't sleep with her anyway. She's too damaged and sex would complicate things." I stared at the steps thinking about what just transpired. I've never cheated on Mecca and here I am in Jersey, exchanging slob and almost having sex with another woman. I need to stay away from her.

"Look at you thinking like a grown man."

"Whatever. Hit me up later for dinner. Just me and you." I kissed her cheek and disappeared out the door.

Ariel Glover

"Don't forget to call your mom." I reminded Armonie as I walked past her door.

After my cousin left yesterday, I stayed downstairs studying for my exam coming up. I'm already an LPN and loved my job but I want to be a RN now. Hell, I'm even taking management classes to be head nurse and the supervisor. Eventually, when I get my foot in the door, I want to run the whole floor and move up higher if I can. My goal is to run a hospital but there's so many steps to go through.

My father Birch is building a small hospital in Monmouth County NJ over in the Fort Monmouth area. Ever since the base closed a few years back, all of the space has been up for sale. Him and my uncle purchased a huge part and once the people heard a hospital and research facility would be there, they had no problem giving it to them. If I want to have a part in it, I want to make sure to provide my degrees if necessary. Whether my family has the money to do whatever, I want everyone to know I took the exact same steps others did.

"Thanks. I spoke to her." She sat on my bed as I finished putting my ankle boots on. VJ wanted to go out for dinner and he's not the type to expect cheap. The restaurant he decided on was hella expensive and the least I could do is dress nice.

"You ok?"

"I wanna leave him Ariel but he won't let me." She busted out crying. I ran over to the bed and rubbed her back.

"Then VJ saved me from his wrath, well before it got worse and things changed." She laid her head on my shoulder.

"What you mean?"

"I know I'm worth so much more but when Haven asked what happened, I begged VJ with my eyes not to mention it, and the look he gave me hurt."

"Hurt?" I questioned.

"It's like he wanted to take me away and I didn't let him. Ariel, I know his mom had a bad relationship and he probably sees me in her, but I don't know how to get out. I've tried and yes it's my fault for accepting the gifts and apologies but he's gonna kill me." Her cries became louder. I went in the bathroom and handed her tissue.

"The only way to end your fear is to tell your family."

"NO!" She shouted.

"Ariel, the Reaper won't have a problem ending him and God forbid Colby Jr. finds out. Sis, you have the means to get rid of Freddy. Why are you saving him?"

"I don't know. I love his mom and family. I know if they kill him, they'll be hurting." I kneeled in front of her.

"I'm not judging Monie because I've never been through this." I took her hand on mine.

"You know when enough is enough, and I understand how you feel towards his family but he's gonna kill you. There's no more saving him and if you don't tell your family, you can be mad all you want, but I will." She forced herself to stand.

"Ariel you're my best friend. How are you gonna tell them when..." She had an attitude and I didn't care. I should've told a long time ago but not betraying her trust, I didn't and now look. The nigga is doing everything to keep her away from the world. Once that happens, we'll never know what's going on.

"When what Monie? When he kills you?" I let her hands go and stood.

"I refused to sit back any longer helping you hide bruises and broken bones from your family. I'm as bad as him and you're putting me in a position to lie. I hate lying to your mom and I feel like your dad can see straight through me." She snickered.

"Don't laugh trick. I be scared as hell when your father questions me." Her father Colby is cool as hell but when it comes to his kids, he don't play.

"How did you feel when VJ was here?" She rolled her eyes.

"I'm asking because you've done more with him then Freddy and you've known him longer." She blushed.

"VJ made me feel safe in that short amount of time in the bathroom. Then, he came to check on me and neither of us expected things to go the way they did. Ariel, I swear if you didn't walk in, I probably would've let him be my first." I smirked.

"He made me body feel things Freddy didn't and I don't know why. I loved the way he touched me and girl, his kiss, whew!" She fanned herself.

"Ok. I don't wanna hear what my cousin does."

"I'm just saying. He made my body hot and I finished myself off when he left." Both of us got a good laugh outta that.

"Well you know he has a girl and you have a man. Don't get caught up in the illusion of you two, until both of you are single."

"VJ has a lot going on and I would never bring him in my drama even though he helped me."

"Handle the Freddy shit before I fake drunk and tell everyone." She tossed a pillow at me on the way out the door.

"Love you. Lock up." I shouted and headed to my car. I saw my ex walking towards me and started to go back inside.

"Ariel?" I ignored him and unlocked my door.

"You too good to speak now?"

"What Eddie? Huh? What could you possibly have to say?" I turned and folded my arms against my chest.

Eddie is the guy I used to date for the last six months. He was cool and fun to be around. It took me the entire six months before deciding to sleep with him. The night I did, of course I went down on him because he did me. We had sex and it was ok, but we had feelings for each other, so I didn't make a big deal out of it. I figured we could explore each other and learn new things together.

The next day, this nigga goes and tells everyone we slept together, and you know how fast shit travels on social media.

Long story short, he's a skinny dude and I'm thick as hell. Some would consider me fat because I'm short like my mom. I'm only 5'5 and I weigh 150 pounds the most. I'm not tryna be a model and I refuse to not eat, to keep up some fake image these girls have online.

Anyway, they made fun of him for sleeping with a fat girl. Instead of defending me, he goes and tells them he wanted to know what it's like to fuck a BBW and I couldn't suck dick for shit. I was so hurt; especially when he was moaning louder than me.

I could've hit him back and showed the messages he sent of how good I made him feel but what for? He already damaged my name which is why Haven calls me the DS ho. Mind you I've only done Eddie and the guy who was my first but let Eddie tell it, I've been around the world and back again doing it to hundreds of men. Yet, here he is begging for me to give him another chance.

"I wish I would fuck with you again on any level. You're childish, petty and can't fuck." He turned his face up.

"Fuck you bitch. Pussy ain't all that." I sat in my car and rolled the window down.

"Says the nigga tryna dive in. Peace." I gave him the peace sign and left him standing there looking stupid.

****

"I'm here for the Davis reservation." I told the hostess at the front door.

"Oh yes. Here it is. Mr. Davis isn't here yet but I can seat you and get you started on a drink."

73

"Thank you." I followed her to the table. She took my drink order and said the waiter would bring it shortly. I glanced over the menu and the prices were high as fuck. Regardless if a person has money or not, food shouldn't cost this much.

"What's up dicksucker?" How ironic is it for us both to be here?

"What the fuck you want Haven?" I peeped the chick next to him and shook my head. She was indeed a bad white chick but why is she here? I know for a fact Juicy's gone and she's the only one he'd bring to an expensive place.

"Go to the table. I'll be right there." The chick listened and he plopped his ignorant ass in the seat.

"You look hungry as hell sitting here alone." I rolled my eyes. He leaned back staring at me. Haven was a handsome dude and the bitches loved him, but his mouth was horrible. He had no filter and gave zero fucks what he said or who he said it to.

"Anything else?" I asked and glanced over the menu. He knew how to get a rise outta me and I was trying not to let him.

74

"Yea. I need my dick sucked later and I was wondering if you're services are available?" I slammed the menu down.

"Haven, I'm starting to think you wanna see what this mouth do." I rolled my tongue inside and he smirked.

"It's about time we on the same page. Look." He turned to make sure no one was listening.

"I'm about to feed this bitch, and then cut her tongue out. Soon as I'm done, be ready." He had no remorse for the lifestyle he had.

"Hold up." I put my hand up and looked around myself.

"Did you just tell me the *Reaper* is on duty right now and to be available when you done?" I whispered.

I know who he is and the only other people who do, are family. He never wanted anyone to associate the two together which is why his identity was always unknown. People knew the so-called reaper is related to the Banks family but could never figure out who it is.

"You've been around long enough to know what it is. But back to the question at hand."

"Haven even if I thought about your disgusting ass proposal why would I do it when you about to fuck her?"

"I always shower after fucking so my dick will be clean. And who the fuck cares. Is every dick you suck clean?"

"The two that I've done, yes they were and stop putting all these men on me." He put his hands up in surrender and stood.

"Play all you want but if I put this dick in your life, I need you to play your position." He said and stood up.

"What?" I had to look up at him.

"I don't want a girlfriend after the shit Juicy did but if the head and pussy good, I'll put you in the top five."

"Bye Haven." This is the shit I be talking about.

"You may have given head a lot but you miss feeling a dick inside you." I shifted in my seat when he said it.

"Bet those panties getting wet." He whispered in my ear and I didn't say anything.

"Let me know when you ready." He placed a kiss on my neck, and I pushed him away. How the hell did he get me wet?

I saw VJ coming my way and tried to remove Haven's remarks from my head but it's gonna be hard with the things he said. I'm damn sure in need of feeling someone inside me and it won't be him.

"Sorry I'm late. Ma, wouldn't let me leave. Talking about I need to take Mecca with me." I peeked around him.

"Where is she?"

"At ya moms house with her."

"VJ how you got her down here and doing other stuff?" He picked the menu up.

"I didn't wanna bring her and we do stuff. I figured since my mom made me, its only fair to let them hang out." I busted out laughing and enjoyed my dinner with him. I couldn't help but sneak a peek at Haven here and there. Dammit! I can not fuck him. Is what my mind is saying, however, my body isn't saying the same.

Haven

"Who is she and why were you talking to her?" The bitch Kathy asked when I sat across from her.

"Are you my girl?" She gave me a look.

"I didn't think so; therefore, who I speak to is none of your got damn business." I lifted the menu and decided on a big juicy steak and mashed potatoes.

"I can't wait to get you in the room. You have no idea how long I've been waiting to share a bed with you." This white bitch was corny as hell. I don't discriminate on who I fuck. Pussy is pussy. Its all about how you work it and if you can have me coming back.

I have yet to hit her off and here she is making dumb ass comments. I could see if we slept together previously or something.

"You better blow my mind since you talking tough." She smiled and did some shit with her tongue. It wasn't as sexy as the way Ariel did it. She had my dick jumping.

"Oh, I will. It's gonna have you begging me to come back." I laughed hard as hell. People were staring; including Ariel. I knew talking nasty would get her panties wet because most women were like that. The only difference is you can't see their clit get hard like you can see a niggas dick.

I smiled the last time she stared at me because it's obvious she's ready for me. Hell yea I fucks with her heavy even though I give her a hard time about the rumors. Whether she goes down on mad niggas or not, she thorough as hell and it helps, she's best friends with my cousin. Her family ain't copasetic so I know she ain't no snitch. Hell, her brother is my best friend so of course he does the same shit.

In any case, I never been attracted to her sexually because honestly, she's not my type. Her body is banging and she never looks a mess but she's my boy's sister and I just don't see us together in any way.

We wouldn't mesh together because I'd probably break her heart and then Armonie would yell and who feels like hearing it. Plus, I know for a fact she won't let me cheat. Juicy knew what it was and allowed it as long as no bitch approached her. Now that I think about it, maybe it's why she cheated. Oh well, she learned you can't do the same thing.

When the dude sat down across from Ariel, I noticed him as the same one who helped Armonie in the bathroom, but who is he? I've never seen him around before and if he's in this town, he needs to know who the fuck I am. Say what you want but I run shit here and ain't no outta town motherfucker coming in tryna pull rank.

I snapped a photo of him and sent it to Colby. He's good as hell in the technology department. He could find out someone's entire life in less than twenty minutes and if I wanted to ruin your credit, he could do that too.

"Let's get outta here. I got shit to do." I slammed the menu down and got up.

"But we never ate." She whined.

"Who cares? You tryna fuck right?" I stared at her.

"Yes but..."

"Then lets go. We can order room service." She followed me as I made a pit stop at Ariel's table.

"I don't give a fuck who you are nigga, but I appreciate you looking out for my cousin." I said to the dude.

"Nice introductions and it's all good. The nigga had no business..." He was about to say something.

BOOM! I heard the dishes on the table clink. Ariel must've kicked him under it, which automatically made my antennas go up.

"The nigga had no business what?" I questioned.

"Look. I don't know what she has going on but you need to check on her." I placed my gaze on Ariel.

"Tha fuck he talking about?"

"Nothing Haven." She couldn't even look at me.

"Yea a'ight. I'll be over later to test those tonsils."

"Yo nigga. Keep it moving with that disrespectful shit." Her cousin stood and we were toe to toe. Three of my boys came rushing over. I didn't travel alone when I'm in the Reaper zone because you never know.

"VJ it's ok. This is how we talk." She pushed him back.

"Well he needs to speak different in my presence. The shit disrespectful and ain't no nigga talking to you like that in front of me." He looked me up and down.

"No nigga." I smirked.

"You heard what I said Ariel." I taunted him to see what he about.

"Oh, you think I'm playing." This nigga got in a fighting stance and I must say, him not being scared or worried intrigued me. Its obvious he has no clue who I am.

"I don't care about how many people you got with you." He glanced over at the dudes who were with me.

"Haven just go." I tossed my toothpick at him and he swung off. I expected it and moved just in time making him catch one of my boys.

"Haven break this up." Ariel yelled.

"You letting me cum down your throat later?"

"What?" She was tryna pull her cousin off who was getting the best of my boy. I mean he was about to kill him.

"You heard me." I gestured with my head for the other two to get in it.

82

"Fine. Just stop this shit." She begged.

"Crybaby." I mushed her in the forehead.

"GET THE FUCK UP!" I barked and my boys stopped.

"Punk ass motherfucker. Letting your boys do the dirty work. Don't worry. Our time is coming."

"Vernon please. Just leave it alone." Ariel pleaded with him and diverted her eyes to me. She knew just like I did, if he continued running his mouth what would happen.

"I'll see you soon." I hit her with the head nod, grabbed the white bitch who was in the corner petrified and left. I'll see him sooner than he thinks; especially now that Colby sent me his information.

****

"That was pretty hectic." Kathy said. I pressed the elevator button and waited for the doors to open.

"What?"

"The fight at the restaurant. I've never been so close to violence." I laughed on the inside because this bitch was really playing her part.

"Go head." I waited for her to step on.

"Yea it's crazy." I said with no emotion.

"Why are we going to the..." I placed my index finger on her lips to cut her off before she could say basement in case the bitch had on a wire.

"This is what you want right?" I held her hand as she stepped off. We walked down the hallway and into a small door leading even lower in the ground. If she is wearing a wire no reception is down here.

Armonie owned this hotel but nobody knew except family. This is where we committed most of our murders. The room we had made is the size of a football field due to all the different machines and weapons. I could describe it but know this is never a place you wanna be. Armonie has only been here once and she hates it. Her exact words were, *do you really need a torture room?* Hell yea we did. Plus, the entire floor is a drain leading into the river. So if cops did raid they wouldn't find any blood or DNA.

"You ready to ride this ride?" I smiled at the fear on her face.

"Ughhh. Yes." I opened the door and vomit escaped her lips instantly.

"You can't be throwing up in here." Jax said and placed a chair in front of her.

"Sit." Her body began to shake and suddenly her bowels escaped down her legs.

"Please."

"Please what?" She looked around the room at her colleagues who were in a chair as well. Two of them were missing arms, two were missing legs but each one no longer had eyes and their ears were removed. I wonder if they can still hear?

"You thought tryna fuck me would give these guys a chance to catch me but I think you forgot who I am." She cried.

"Had you remembered you'd know before you and your team even thought of the plan, I was already five steps ahead of you."

"But how?"

"The captain is a friend of mine and well, he couldn't stand you. Therefore, he set you up on a case he'd know you lose your life over." I'm still waiting on the captain to tell me who put a bug in their ear because they never bother me.

"Please don't do this." I put some gloves on, took the tongs out Jax hand and tilted her head.

"We can do this the easy way or the hard way."

"What?"

"Stick your tongue out." She closed her mouth tight as she could. I nodded to Jax and Brayden who walked over and used some hooks to pry her mouth open. Kathy tried shaking her head no but the grip I had on her was serious.

"This is for running your mouth about investigating me." I pulled her tongue out with the tongs, switched hands with Jax so he could hold her head and sliced her tongue off. The scream was expected and so was the fainting. Most people can't take extreme pain.

"My turn." Brayden stood in front of her with a chainsaw and took all four of her limbs off. I turned and stared at her husband who shit on himself too.

"When you get to hell beat her ass for getting you mixed up with her shit." I told him.

"You won't get away with this." I let a grin come across my face.

"The Reaper gets away with everything." His eyes got big.

"You know the name." He nodded.

"Good." I jammed a screwdriver in his ear hard as I could and watched him jerk. I loved death.

"I'm out." I left the tool in his head and removed my gloves to toss in the incinerator.

"I want this room spotless in five minutes." I told the clean-up guys. I never wasted time making things look normal. When you do, it gives people a chance to slack off and get you caught. It may be our torture room but it's under my cousin's name. I'd never put her in harms way.

Armonie

"Are you going to ever tell me what happened? There's no way you fell into a wall at the club." My mom rubbed my head.

After the night Freddy put his hands on me again, VJ stopped by and gave me the same erotic kiss he gave his girl at the club and I swear, he could've been my first at that very moment.

The following day, Ariel said I had to inform my family, or she would. As I stare in my mother's eyes, I just couldn't. She'd probably cry and send every guy in my family after him. I'm just gonna stay away from Freddy and hopefully he'll catch the hint.

Once the doctor discharged me from the hospital, I checked on him. VJ fractured his jaw and that's not even discussing the black eyes, split nose and cracked ribs. I didn't see the fight, or should I say beatdown, because after tossing me like a rag doll, I was knocked out.

His mom asked if I were ok because she saw the bandage on my head. I wanted to tell her too but kept my mouth shut. I don't even know why I'm saving him at this point because he's not going to stop.

"I was tipsy ma and fell. Ariel's cousin is the one who helped me." I lied with a straight face.

"Why did he beat Freddy up?"

"I have no idea. Did you cook?" I asked tossing the covers off my legs. I've been here for a few days trying to avoid Freddy's wrath because I know he's gonna blame me for VJ whooping his ass. I wish I could've seen it.

"Yea. Your dad and brother are down there too and I'm sure they'll have questions." I hopped my ass right back in the bed.

"Can you bring me a plate?"

"No. Get down there and deal with them." I pouted.

"Armonie what's going on with you? I don't know why but it seems like the energetic, strong child I had is shutting down. It's like you're in a shell."

"I don't know ma. I'm just tired of discussing the club thing."

"I understand honey but it's way too many men in this family for it to be pushed under the rug." She ran her hand down my face.

"When you're ready to reveal the truth, I'll be right here." I nodded and rose from the bed.

"I pray you're not allowing him to put his hands on you." I swallowed hard and lied again.

"Not at all." She and I went downstairs and joined the rest of the family for dinner. It wasn't too bad and no one questioned me.

My brother Colby and father definitely knew I was hiding something because each of them said, when the truth comes out, if it's bad no one will be able to escape their wrath. My family are a bunch of savages and it's the reason why the girls in our family are always scared to date.

****

"Hey girl. You tryna hit the hair salon with me?" Ariel asked when she stopped by. My aunt Venus runs six shops in different areas and loved when we came in. She shows all of us off and even claims Ariel as her niece since she's been around forever.

"I guess. Let me grab my sneakers." I went in the other room and picked everything up I needed to go.

"You ready?" I asked. She was speaking to my mom about coloring her hair.

"Yup." She gave my mother a hug and we left.

On the way over she started telling me how she hopes she passed all the exams she's been taking. I applauded her hard work because she was in school and worked twelve hour shifts four days a week. Like the rest of us, she didn't have to but did it anyway.

"Hey my boo's. Ariel go straight to the sink and Armonie you do the same." My aunt Venus said and walked to the other side of the salon to check on a woman under the dryer.

"Are you coloring your hair Ariel?" The two of them started talking as I searched the hair magazine for a new style.

I couldn't find one I liked so I'm just gonna get it washed, dried and wrapped like usual.

BING! BING! Everyone looked at the door.

"DAMN! Who man is he?" Some woman yelled out. I couldn't help but smile because he was sexy as fuck to me.

"Mine." Ariel and I turned our head. We didn't even know the Mecca bitch was here.

"You sure because he on his way to them." The woman was being messy.

"That's his cousin." You could hear Mecca answering but I had my eyes on VJ. He was dressed to impress, and a bitch was fantasizing about that kiss.

"What up y'all?"

"Hey." I waved and he leaned down to kiss Ariel's cheek. He stood me up and hugged me.

"You want another kiss don't you?" He whispered in my ear. I was about to answer but his nagging ass girlfriend came over.

"I get why you hugging your cousin but she don't need no hug. Why you hugging her?" She crossed her arms and VJ turned around.

"How much is your hair?" He ignored her question.

"Seventy-five and you still didn't answer."

"And I'm not because I'm a grown ass man. Now go to the register and I'll be right there." She stormed off.

"Damn girl. He got that ass in check." Some woman said.

"Whatever." Mecca said.

"And don't get up until he tells you too." The women were clowning her and I had to stifle my own laugh.

"Why can't I stop thinking about the kiss?" He asked and moved his mouth by my ear.

"If we weren't attached, I'd take your ass home with me." He backed away, licked his lips and headed over to Mecca.

"Bitch, I'ma need to know what the fuck he said." Ariel stood in front of me and so did my aunt Venus.

"Ughhh."

"Ugh, my ass. You better tell aunty what's going on." My aunt took me in the back room with Ariel and closed the door.

"Nothing aunt Venus, He stopped by, we kissed, and he said if we weren't attached, he'd wanna take me home."

"Oh shit bitch. Let me find the fuck out." Ariel said and smirked.

"Well, he don't look too attached to his bitch." My aunt opened the door and you could see VJ walking out the salon while she grabbed her things.

"If you get the chance again, take him from her." My aunt had me cracking up.

"You know I'm still a virgin so I wouldn't have any idea what to do. And don't forget he lives in Virginia."

"Girl bye. I95 goes straight there." Me and Ariel were cracking up. My aunt sent us back in and had us sit at the sink.

"I see how you look at my man but he's hands off." Mecca said standing in front of me.

"Ariel, do you hear anything?"

"Nope."

"Well hear this." Mecca came closer and I sat up in the chair. I saw my aunt speed walking over to us.

"If I find out you coming on to my man, it'll be hell to pay. Ahhhhh!" She shouted when my aunt pulled her by the hair.

"Take your dumb ass the fuck up outta here and before you question a woman about the man you're supposed to be with, have your facts straight." Mecca didn't say anything.

"A man and woman can flirt all they want but until something happens, all it is, is flirting. Also, you need to tell your man to keep his distance because as you can see, he approached her, not the other way around. Bye." My aunt pushed her out the store and everyone busted out laughing. My aunt Venus don't play when it comes to family either.

After we finished at the hair salon, we picked up some take out and went back to the apartment. I decided to give my parents a break and stay at my own place. They don't mind but I'm tired of the stares.

"What up?" VJ said when I opened the front door. I looked around him to see if she was with him.

"She not here. I needed a break. What y'all got to eat?"

"Hey VJ." Ariel spoke from the living room as I closed the door. I went to my spot on the other end of the couch.

"I'm gonna need a meal next time I stop by." He yelled from the kitchen.

"We didn't know you were coming." Ariel and I focused on the scary movie we were watching, and he plopped down in between us.

"Where y'all men at?" He asked eating some leftovers.

"You know I don't have one." Ariel smacked his arm and he looked at me.

"We're taking a break." I shrugged and he gave me a confused look.

"I don't wanna talk about it." He left it alone and the three of us finished watching the movie together. When it was over, we smoked some weed with him and joked around for the next few hours. It felt good not worrying about anything. If only my life was this carefree everyday.

By the time VJ left it was after two in the morning. His chick is gonna be mad as hell. I wish I could be a fly on the wall, just to be petty.

Christian

"How's grams baby doing?" My grandmother took lil Christian out my hand when she opened the door. Here we are at another Sunday dinner but this time without my wife.

After leaving the church not too long ago and letting her know not to mess with my family, she returned to the house in full bitch form. I mean she was screaming and acting crazy like someone was killing her. If one thing my mom taught me, it's to record every detail of a scorned woman. She may not be scorned because I never cheated on her but she's definitely upset about me mentioning the divorce.

Anyway, she started breaking things in the house, tossing my stuff out on the yard and yelling about me not taking my son. I had to remind her the house is in my name and she's only a visitor. I tried to calm her down and have a civilized conversation, but she refused.

Before anyone flips, her dumb ass mother told her not to get on the deed. Talking about if I ever left her, she'd be responsible for the mortgage and everything else. It would mess up her credit. I know she dumb as hell.

After I put my son to sleep that night, I cleaned the house, showered and went downstairs. Why did I overhear her on the phone discussing the divorce with her mother? I expected it but what I didn't expect is her mother explaining how Elaina needed to give me more sex and even offer up a threesome. I've never indulged in one even though my brother and cousins swear they're the best thing popping.

And sex with my wife is a no go at this point. I don't need any more kids or complications with her. It's sad because she tried to suck my dick a few days ago and I couldn't get hard, which was a clue that I'm truly over her and this marriage. Something I never thought could happen.

"He's good. You think we can stay here until I get a new place?" She popped me upside my head.

"All my grandkids are welcomed here. Don't ever disrespect me and ask no dumb question like that again." I kissed her cheek and reached in the fridge for a soda.

"Hey baby." My mom walked in and hugged me. She was a worry wort and assumed I was devastated about the divorce. I may have been if it happened two years ago. However, it's been a long time coming.

"Hey. Where's pops?" She gave me a dirty look. It only meant he's outside smoking. She worshipped the ground my father walked on and vice versa but she hated the fact he smokes all the time.

My aunts don't really care about my uncles doing it but like I said, my mom is a worry wort. She thinks one day the FDA is gonna say weed is causing cancer or something. I smiled and walked outside with him. Haven was with him and so was Armonie, Jax, Colby Jr and my uncles. When the hell did they all get here?

"What up divorcee?" Armonie said and kissed my cheek.

"You think Grams would mind if Stormy stopped by?" All conversations stopped.

"It's about time you gonna get some new pussy. She bad too bro." Haven responded before anyone.

"She has a man." I told them and sent a message to Stormy saying she could stop by.

"And you have a wife. Who the fuck cares? You two been tryna fuck for years." Jax said.

"Stop playing and take her in one of those extra rooms." Colby Jr. chimed in.

"She better be screaming too bro or I'm disowning yo ass." Haven had jokes.

"He only asked her to come over. Damn y'all. But son she better make some sorta noise if you take her in the room." My father said and I left all them out there. I loved my family but sometimes they're too much.

****

"Hey everybody." I heard Stormy's voice as we sat down to eat. She gave everyone a hug and disappeared with Armonie. Those two were cool.

"Give me my grandson." Grams reached out for him.

"He's good."

"Boy get your ass in there with Stormy." My father yelled as the entire family made plates.

"Whatever." I went on the back porch where the two women were and interrupted their conversation.

"Talk to you later Stormy." Armonie smirked walking away.

"Hey you." I didn't bother speaking, grabbed her hand and went in the house.

"YEA NIGGA!" Haven yelled.

"Huh?" Stormy was confused as she should be.

I opened a bedroom door, closed it and threw Stormy against the back of it. Nothing about this is right but I had to have her. Ever since we almost kissed in my office, she's been heavy on my mind. I wanted to call her but it wouldn't have been right. It must be meant for us to be here if she text me, right?

"Christian what are you..." I cut her off with a kiss. She let her arms draped around my neck as I felt all over her chest.

"Slow down Christian." She moved me away and started disposing of her clothes. Images of her body would forever be in my head.

The way her breasts sat up after she unhooked the bra and the perfect shave down below. My heart was racing with anticipation. It could be because I've never encountered sex with another woman and now I am with my family only yards away.

"I'm not sure how you used to have sex with your wife but let me show you how to please me." She took my hands, placed them on her breasts and had me rubbed them slow.

"Suck on them Christian." She held them in my face, and I took each one in my mouth. Flickering both nipples and making sure to give each one the same amount of attention.

"It feels good." I lifted her up and gently laid her on the bed.

"I know how to make love to a woman Stormy. I just got a little excited. Its my first time with another lady." I took my clothes off and kissed her body from head to toe.

"Oh God." She all but screamed when I inserted my tongue in her pussy.

"You like this?" I questioned by placing my finger in her ass at the same time she succumbed to the first orgasm.

"Yes Christian, yes." She began grinding on my face and in one instant, came so hard I had to cover her mouth due to the pleasure making her scream. I kissed back up her body and stopped.

"You ok?" I was about to enter another woman and had no bad feeling whatsoever.

"Yea." I entered her and the feeling was different and amazing. The two of us continued sexing each other down with no cares in the world. I did have to make her scream a few times so my brother and cousins could hear. I don't need them clowning me and saying she was too quiet.

"I'm about to cum Stormy." I sucked on the side of her neck as our bodies were in a doggy style position.

"Ok." She jumped off my dick and it felt like I was getting blue balls. I was about to say something until she pushed me back and got on her knees.

"Got damn." I put the palm of my hand on top of her head and pump in and out her mouth. Elaina has never sucked me off this good. When she swallowed, I lost it and caught myself from falling. She stood and both of us stared.

"I need a shower. You coming?" She asked walking ahead of me in the adjoining bathroom.

"Hell yea." I followed and indulged in more sex. By the time we came out everyone was finished eating and talking or lounging around.

"Two hours. My nigga." Colby Jr. walked past us on the phone. Stormy put her head down as we walked in the kitchen.

"I made your plates." My mom sat them in front of us and smiled.

"I know you're getting a divorce son but Stormy please make sure the man you're dealing with doesn't approach my son." She nodded and the two of us dug in.

"I'm breaking up with him." She was texting away on her phone.

"We can't have any more sex until you're fully unattached." I didn't want her sleeping with the both of us. Tonight, I wanted it as bad as she did.

"I agree but it means no sex with anyone else either." She responded.

"After those freaky things you did to me, I don't want no one else." We busted out laughing.

Stormy had me trying things on her Elaina would turn her face up at. It's all good because it's more things I wanna do and since I know she's down, heck yea I'm doing them with her.

"Am I allowed to join the party? I mean we are still married." I saw Stormy's body tense up.

"Why are you here?" Elaina made her way around the island to stand in front of us.

"The baby and I are hungry." She rubbed her stomach and I dropped my fork. I lost my appetite.

Stormy

Sex with Christian was exactly how I imagined it to be. Amazing and exhausting. At first, I thought he'd be boring, and I'd have to guide him. When he took over, all the fantasies I had between the two of us came true. The freaky sex, how he ate my pussy and the way he made love to me. It's no way in hell he sexed his wife the same and she still wasn't happy.

He was absolutely right about us not engaging in anymore sex until I break up with Curtis. It would complicate things; especially if we wanted to explore being in a relationship. It couldn't happen if I'm with him. That's why I sent him a text saying we needed to talk. It shouldn't be a problem because he's never home anyway. Do I think he's cheating? I know he's cheating and has been for a while, which is why I no longer go to his house. I'm too nervous about walking in on something.

He didn't respond to the text like I expected so I sent him another one saying we'd talk whenever he feels like it. Again, there was no response and I didn't even care. Christian was here and the two of us seemed right. I couldn't wait to be his woman and let everyone know. The congregation wanted him to get rid of his wife and find someone else. I'm not sure how they'll react to us, but my parents will love it. They love them some Christian Banks and my mom always hinted around to us being a couple.

I guess Christian finally listened because he filed for divorce; yet this bitch is standing here announcing a pregnancy. I'm a tad bit upset but she's his wife; therefore, it's a possibility and most likely happened before we crossed the line.

The look of aggravation and anger plagued Christian's face as I sat there witnessing another argument between them.

"How many months are you?" He asked.

"This is a husband and wife conversation, you can excuse yourself." Elaina snapped at me. I stood and Christian grabbed my hand.

"She's not finished eating. Stay right here Stormy." I smirked and placed my ass in the seat.

"Christian she doesn't need to be in our business. It's bad enough she knows about our divorce." She pouted.

"Everyone knows about the divorce because you couldn't keep your mouth shut. Telling your mother, who in return, told anyone who would listen. If you wanna blame anyone for finding out, blame yourself and her." I could tell he was about to go in on her.

"It's ok Christian. I had a fun, and exhausting night. It's like my body succumb to extensive pleasure and needs to rest." He smirked.

"I'll be right back." He told Elaina and walked me to my car.

"Why is that bitch here?" His grams asked smoking with the guys in the driveway.

"I was gonna ask who let her in." He said.

"She probably let herself in. You know grams leaves the door unlocked. Call me later Stormy." Armonie yelled out.

"You ok?" Christian asked opening the car door.

"We're not together and it's before my time. No more sex right?" He smiled.

"Not with her." I leaned it to kiss him and he happily accepted. It made me wonder if his wife was paying attention. It didn't matter because he damn sure had no problem doing it.

"Let me go before I ask you to leave with me." He shook his head.

"Text me when you get home." He pecked my lips again and closed the door. I pulled out the driveway and laughed as his cousins and brothers gave him a pound on his way in the house. His family are comical.

****

"What about your girlfriend?" I sat behind Curtis in a separate booth at the bar. I followed him from his house after he claimed to be working late.

The day after sleeping with Christian, I called my man and asked if we could meet for breakfast. As usual he was busy and promised to see me at night. The night came and left and no sign of Curtis. It was excuse after excuse for the next few days. I mentioned breaking up because he had no time for me, and his ass flipped. Talking about I'm not respecting his job hours and blah, blah, blah. I had the key to his house but like I

110

said, I'm not walking into him possibly having sex with another woman. Nope. I won't do it to myself.

Here I am sitting with Armonie deciding if I should inform him of my existence. She's ready to beat the woman up, where I'm happy to catch him out there. In three years, our relationship has run its course and it won't be any love lost here. I was ok not telling him and moving on because he obviously is, but my father said it's not right and to do it the grown up way.

"I barely see her and I told you we don't have sex. You're the woman I want. Why can't you see it? I'm with you damn near 24/7." That's all I needed to hear.

"Hey Curtis." I swore the blood drained from his face.

"Thank you." I looked at the woman who had no idea why I was thanking her.

"Excuse me!"

"Thank you for exposing Curtis for the lying, cheating asshole he really is."

"Stormy." He tried to get up.

"Stormy? This is your girlfriend?" She pointed to me.

"Correction. Was his girlfriend." I turned to look at him.

"Curtis, I mentioned breaking up and you forbid it. What I don't understand is why when you've clearly moved on." He went to stand and I put my hand up.

"Save it. Have a good life." I told Armonie to move our seats and she agreed. Curtis stormed out leaving the chick sitting in the booth. Exactly what she gets for knowing he had a woman and stayed around.

"Now you and my cousin can finally hook up?" She sounded excited.

"He has to deal with the wife."

"Wife? That bitch got cursed out when you left by all of us."

"What? Why?" I wanted to know details.

"Girl. She tried to throw a fake pregnancy on Christian."

"Fake?" I was confused.

"Yup. Little did she know my grams had pregnancy tests under her bathroom sink." I almost choked on my drink.

"Why does your grandmother have tests under her sink?" I used a napkin to wipe my mouth.

"Who knows? She said if any of my brothers or cousins gets a chick pregnant, they need to prove it. She makes sure to have updated ones too." I fell out laughing.

"How are you doing?" I asked and she shrugged her shoulders before asking the bartender for two patron shots.

"I'm over Freddy."

"Are you?" I gave her the side eye because she's been saying it for a while now and still with him.

"I am. He's no longer the man I thought he was. Everything about us being together is wrong."

"What you mean?" She told me to hold on and gulped down the two shots. The bartender placed two margaritas in front of her.

"He's only staying with me because of my V status. My grandmother says he wants me to be strung out on my first sexual experience, that way I'll never leave him."

"Girl bye. These days women could care less about their first sexual experience. Yes, some have good luck and others don't. However, it doesn't necessarily mean the woman would be stuck."

"I know right. FUCK FREDDY!" She shouted and drank her margarita.

"Remember the VJ guy I mentioned?" A smile came across her face.

"Yea." I do remember her mentioning him.

"Well, we kissed and he had me feeling things I've never felt before."

"Really?" She spoke highly of the guy and I was happy for her. The only question is, will Freddy let her go. We sat there talking for a little while and I could tell she was over her ex, but she's staying around for some reason.

"Ok lady. Let me get you home." I told her after noticing how tipsy she is. She stood and almost hit the ground. When we looked up, some sexy ass man was staring down at her. Lord, she doesn't need to meet anyone else.

V J

"Where you going?" Mecca asked the second my foot hit the threshold.

"Out." I had plans on going to this nigga Haven's club and approaching him about the shit with my cousin Ariel. I don't give a fuck how much they play, he needs to respect her.

When we left, she explained how they spoke to one another and I get it. However; she should respect herself more than to allow him to do it in public. I don't care how long they've known one another. My mom would kick my ass if she heard me speak to a woman that way and Brayden would be ready to fight if he knew she allowed it. Whatever the case he's gonna see me.

"Out where and you didn't ask me."

"Mecca not right now." I left her sitting there and went to shower. This shit is nowhere near over between me and the Haven dude. Who cares that I swung off first, he had no business talking crazy to Ariel.

"Babe, your cousin Brayden is here." She yelled in the bathroom.

"Tell him I'll be right down." I heard the door close and finished washing up. I put my clothes on and grabbed what I needed to go.

"What up?" I said when I walked downstairs.

"Shit. Where you going?" He asked and walked out the door with me.

"To find this dude."

"What dude?" He became defensive and ready to fight.

"Haven. You know him?" Brayden stopped and stared.

"Why you looking for him?" I explained what went down and he shook his head laughing,

"What's so funny?"

"Ok, first off that's my boy and second, didn't Ariel tell you its how they speak to one another?" He questioned and leaned against the car with me.

"First, I don't care if he's your boy and second you're ok with the way he speaks to her?"

116

"You've been gone a long time cousin. Let me fill you in real quick."

"Fill me in then because this don't make no sense."

"Haven and Ariel fucks with each other heavy." I looked at him.

"Believe it or not, they do. He appreciates how thorough she is and how she has Armonie's back at all times. Do he say fucked up shit? Absolutely but its how he talks." I went to talk and he put his hand up.

"It may not be something you or I would do but if Ariel told him he was being disrespectful, he'd stop. If you ask me, I think he's feeling her but he also knows if they ever took it there Ariel wouldn't allow him to cheat on her like his ex did." All I could do is shake my head.

"I'm not saying what he says to her is ok, and I approached her about it a few times. Haven may be my boy, but she's my sister."

"What did Ariel say?"

"She told me not to worry about it because she can handle him. I backed off and to this day, she has never come to me about him being disrespectful."

"What would you do if she did?" He gave me the side eye. I wasn't implying he was scared of his friend but I wanted to make sure there was some sort of loyalty to family.

"Then I'ma talk to him and if he still did it, then we'd be some beefing motherfuckers." He shrugged his shoulders.

"I know you wanna save all the women in our family just like the rest of us, but Ariel is stronger than you think and can hold her own."

"Whatever. Tell your friend don't do that shit around me or we'll be fighting. I don't care who he bring." He started laughing.

"I miss you cuz. When you coming back?" We embraced one another.

"I only came because your aunt and uncle made me, well asked. Talking about I never come. You know throwing the guilt trip on me."

"I asked them to." I lifted my head from rolling the blunt.

"I need my cousin here to help me run this shit my pops is making me do."

"Huh?" I was confused.

"Pops wants me to run all these places so him and my mom can finally travel. I ain't tryna do that shit and since you've been doing it all this time, why not do it here with me?"

"Hold up nigga. You tryna get me to run it, while you out there doing whatever?" Brayden loved the streets. He'll tell you its his calling.

"I'm saying. I don't know what I'm doing so of course you'll have to teach me but if I'm needed in the streets, I'm out." I laughed at his ass.

"I'll think about it. You know Mecca there and I run the buildings in VA with Vanity."

"Who moving up here too." I looked at him because no one told me.

"Say what?"

"Maybe if you answer when she calls, instead of running around with your chick, you'd know her dude brought her a house out here."

"Whatever. Vanity don't be wanting shit."

"Well, your mom is happy and begging your dad to move here too. And we all know aunt Maylan gets whatever she wants, just like my mom." Both of us couldn't stop laughing.

"We'll see. I need to look at properties and…"

"I got you already."

"What?"

"There are some brand-new houses being built, courtesy of pops and I told him you wanted one."

"Oh so you had this set up." He cheesed hard as hell.

"Everyone on board but you. Think about it." He looked down at his phone and started grinning.

"Wifey calls. I gotta go." We hugged again and promised to meet up tomorrow. I loved visiting Jersey once in a blue moon, but do I really feel like moving here? I hopped in my car and drove to the nigga's club. I'm not gonna say shit

120

now that I spoke with Brayden, but his spot is nice, and I need a drink.

****

"Armonie you know if he catches you here it's gonna be a problem." I turned around and saw her sitting with another beautiful woman. They really did hang in packs.

"Fuck Freddy. He can't tell me what to doooo." She slurred her speech and almost fell off the chair. I knew then, she was tore up or almost there.

I was in the next booth listening to Armonie go on and on about leaving the dude. At one point, she spoke about killing him before he killed her. It's sad when death is the only way outta relationships. If it ain't working, leave. I don't get it.

"Excuse us." The other woman said when they walked by. Monie had fallen in front of me and the second our eyes locked she smiled.

"Still fine as hell." She slurred and the woman stared at me.

"Who are you?"

"Vernon. You good Monie?"

"I am now." She stood and dropped in my lap.

"Umm." The woman didn't know what to say.

"She good. What's your name?" I asked because Monie had her face in the crook of my neck.

"Stormy."

"I got her Stormy."

"Yea he got me Stormy. This is Ariel's cousin. The one I told you who had me soaking wet down there. Can you make me feel like that again Vernon?" Stormy covered her mouth.

"I'll make sure she gets home safe." I winked and Stormy didn't move.

"Call Ariel and get my information if you don't trust me."

"I'm good Stormy. He's where I wanna be." Monie started kissing my neck.

"You sure?"

"I'm sure." She told her and Stormy walked away. Armonie put her knees on the side of me and started unbuttoning her shirt. I stopped her.

"You don't want me either?"

"Monie this ain't the place..." I went to speak and she stood up, grabbing me with her. I carried her out because the way her legs wobbled, she was about to hit the ground.

"Take care of her." Stormy waved with a smile on her face. I placed Monie in the car and started to drive in the direction of her house.

"Hotel Embassy."

"Huh?" She was giving me directions and we ended up in front of this nice ass hotel.

"Pull around the back." I did like she asked and helped her out the car. She used her key to open the door and walked down a hall in a different direction of the regular rooms.

When she opened the door, it was like a damn apartment. There was an upstairs, full living room with a big ass flat screen, a kitchen and dining room. She threw her shoes across the room and walked up the stairs. I made sure the door was locked and followed. It was nicer up here and the bed had to be a California king.

"Thanks VJ for making sure I'm good. That's twice you saved me." She stood on the bed looking down at me.

"I didn't save you tonight although you are pretty fucked up." I could smell the alcohol on her breath even with the mint she popped on the way over.

"I'll never be sloppy drunk, and I just needed something to take the edge off. I have so much going on in my life that it helps." We stared at one another. She leaned in for a kiss and I had every intention of breaking the kiss, but I couldn't. This woman had a hold on me.

Our tongues danced with each other for a few minutes making both of us become aroused. She stopped, lifted the shirt over her head and unhooked the bra. Her breast spilled out and I had to suck on them.

"It feels good Vernon." She rubbed my head as I did it.

"Get down." I lifted her off the bed and took my time removing her clothes. Her body was beautiful.

"We're about to enter a dangerous ground Armonie." She nodded and bit down on her bottom lip.

I gently laid her on the bed, took my shirt off and ran one of my hands up her leg. Goosebumps appeared and her nipples began to harden. I slid my tongue in between her legs and sucked on both thighs. Her wetness was already seeping between her bottom lips and I hadn't even touched her there.

I used my finger to circle her oversized treasure and watched her succumb to a powerful orgasm. Not giving her a chance to catch her breath, I latched on and assaulted her pussy with my tongue. Her back became arched and her knees were up against my head and shaking. I slid one finger inside and curved it.

"Oh shit." She moaned out making my dick harder.

"I don't know what's happening, but I love it. Oh shitttttt." She yelled and her fluids shot right in my mouth. The pulsating could be felt as I stayed put and she experienced two more.

When I finished, it took me a minute to remove all my clothes because I remembered Ariel mentioning her virgin status. Did I wanna be her first? Better yet, did she want me to be?

"I'm ok VJ. I want this." How did she know what I was thinking?

"Monie." I thought about discussing it with her until she slid to the end of the bed and stroked my man with both hands.

"I'm good ma." I was about to push her away because she's a virgin and most likely had no idea what to do. But somehow, she deep throated me. I'm no small nigga and once she hummed on the tip, I couldn't make her get up.

I stared down at her and even tho she gagged here and there, she was doing the damn thing. I guided her at times, and not once did she complain. A fast learner and what made it better was she accepted the help I gave. Its like she wanted to make sure she pleased me, and she did.

"Monie, I can't let you go out like that. I'm about to cum. Get up." Her eyes met mine. She didn't move and actually went faster pulling my nut up.

"Oh fuck!" I snatched her up after I came and in that moment, we were lost in each other.

"This can't happen again." I told her and she shook her head.

"This one night is fine with me." She scooted back on the bed and gestured me with her finger.

"It's our secret Monie."

"Always." I kissed inside her thighs and went down on her again. When she came, I pushed my way in quick. It's the only way to get it over with.

"You ok?" I kissed the couple of tears leaving her eyes.

"I am now." We engaged in a deep and passionate kiss. Her legs wrapped around my back and I drilled deeper.

"Vernon." She moaned out and the sound was perfect.

"Are you making love to me?" I had one of her legs in the air as I moved in circles.

"There's no other way to be with you sexually. Fucking ain't it and after the shit you been through, you deserve the best." She smiled and I got fuzzy inside. What the hell is this woman doing to me?

"Turn over." It took her a minute and I hated to change positions being her first time, but I wanted her to experience every one. I kissed her neck, then down her spine before arching her back and inserting myself in.

I had to close my eyes because she felt so good. Her pussy gripped my dick and had a nigga about to cry from the feeling. I explained how to throw it back and her ass bounced just the way I liked.

"You ready to learn how to ride?" I had her hair entangled in my hand, still hitting it from the back. My other hand was circling get clit.

"Right after I..." Her body shook as another orgasm ripped through her. Who knew a virgin could cum as much as experienced women? I gave her a minute and pulled out.

"Oh my gawwwd." She shouted when I mounted her on top. Her nails were in my chest, but she wasn't digging.

"If it's too much we can stop."

"No. Give me a minute to adjust." I watched her get comfortable and instructed her on what to do. Once she got the hang of it, nothing could stop her.

128

"I'm about to cum Monie." We had been at it for two hours now and even though she was in pain, she refused to stop. Not once did her pussy dry up either.

I had her riding me cowgirl style as I sat on the edge of the bed. My hands were caressing her breasts from behind and her nails were in my legs. I lifted her up and slammed her down over and over. All you heard was the two of us moaning and our skin smacking.

"Come on baby. Cum for me." She said and leaned back so my chest was connected to her back. She moved the hair out her face and turned to kiss me.

"Right there Vernon." I went harder underneath.

"Yes baby." She cried. I circled her clit and a few minutes later we both released. I fell back on the bed with her doing the same. She moved over and my soft dick slid outta her. What the fuck did I just do?

Armonie

I stared at the end of the bed at VJ with his head in his hands. The bare upper half of him showed and I smirked at the barely noticeable scratches I left behind during our indiscretion. We both had other people in our lives, yet, we indulged in adulterous behavior. We may not be married but we both took part in the infidelity.

"You a'ight?" This is the second time he asked post making love to me. I'm assuming it's what we did because there was no rushing, fucking me fast or keeping his eyes closed so he wouldn't look at me. Everything about the way he handled my body is nothing like I expected. It's like he wanted to be with me and made sure to please every single part.

"I'm ok." I sorta lied. I was ok mentally but physically my pussy was sore as hell. I didn't even wanna get up to use the bathroom.

"I'm not in love with her." He said outta the blue.

"I'm not in love with him anymore either." I stared into the darkness thinking about the revelation I said out loud.

The whole time Freddy and I been together it's always been crazy. I thought I was in love until after a month or two it became about sex. When I didn't give him any, he stepped out. I thought it was my fault and took him back. Everything was perfect and I had no worries about our relationship. We were always together and the whole world knew about us. Still I couldn't allow him to be my first.

In the last seven or eight months, he's become violent. I get he wants to be my first sexual experience but why you fighting me? What's the reason for the abuse? I can't fully blame him because I stayed around. I've had a broken arm, black eye and quite a few busted lips; yet nothing or no one could make me leave him.

That is until Vernon came around. I know he has a woman but hearing him say I deserve better, changed my outlook on how a man is supposed to treat me. I'm sad to admit, I thought Freddy loved me and the abuse is part of it. You know he'd come to the house with gifts and I felt special. I figured he was having a bad day and each time he swore it wouldn't happen again.

Here I lay down with another man who I've known growing up and still don't really know him. He treated me with respect and regardless of us indulging in some great sex, we were wrong and like he said, it can never happen again.

"You should go. She's probably waiting on you." He turned to me. Even with just the television on and the moonlight from the window, I could still see how handsome he was.

"You're right but there's a few things left you need to experience before I go." A grin came across my face.

"Oh yea?" He moved the covers off my legs and carried me in the bathroom.

"I'd say a shower but I'm sure you're sore." I laid my head on his shoulder.

"Jacuzzi sex is the bomb." He turned it on and helped me in. I sat on his lap facing him.

"You're worth more than the way you've been treated." I shied away from his gaze.

"Thanks." He tilted my head up and pressed his lips on mine.

"Bend over." He had me stand, turn around in front of him, spread my ass cheeks and ate my pussy from the back. If I thought the regular way was good, this feeling put me on another level. I came so hard he had to catch me from falling head first in the jacuzzi.

"Now let me show you some other things." He pulled me closer and the two of us went at it all night or should I say until I tapped out. This man had me in the jacuzzi, on the kitchen floor, and spread out on the dining room table as he sat in a chair to give me head. I felt like I was in a gyn office. When I say he turned me the fuck out, it's exactly what he did.

By the time I opened my eyes he was gone. I wasn't even mad and wholeheartedly enjoyed my night.

I reached over for my phone and realized it was four in the afternoon. I had tons of missed calls from my family. I sent all of them a text saying I went out last night and slept in.

I sat the phone on the nightstand and reminisced about the things that took place in this very room. I wondered if it would ever happen again and if not, I had a lotta memories to cherish when it comes to my first time. I tossed the covers back and slowly moved my legs so I could leave.

"Owwww." I shouted out loud to no one. My pussy was sore but so worth the pain.

****

"Bitch where you been? Got everyone calling me looking for you."

"I just needed some time away. The shit with Freddy and leaving him is bothering me." I moved past Ariel without looking in her face. She always knew when I was lying, and I promised VJ it would be our secret.

"Yea well. The nigga showed up here and I told him you were at your parents." I turned around.

"I told him to give me some time. Damn he don't listen."

"Armonie, he's not going to let you go. Again, you need to tell someone. Shit, VJ almost mentioned it to Haven the night we saw him at the restaurant."

"What?"

"Yea. I forgot to tell you because you were sleep when I got here and I left before you got up." I told her to give me a minute to change and I'll be down to talk.

I hopped in the shower, threw some sweats on and checked my body for passion marks. Vernon sucked me from head to toe and I wasn't sure if he left any. Not that I'd mind but if Freddy is stopping by, I don't need him trying to kill me before I found a way to tell my family. I shouldn't care what happens to him but when you've been with someone this long, you tend to care.

I walked down the steps and overheard a voice I didn't expect to. Walking into the living room there stood Vernon with his woman. I ping of jealousy shot through my body, but I didn't say a word. I spoke and walked in the kitchen hoping no one noticed the difference in my walk. I damn sure did because I could barely keep my legs closed.

"Are you coming back?" Ariel asked and hugged him. The girlfriend was rolling her eyes.

"Maybe in a few months. I have things that need to be taken care of down there."

"You leaving already Vernon? I thought you and your boo were thinking about getting a place up here." I smirked when no one was looking.

"Maybe later. Right now isn't a good time." He kept his eyes on me.

"I'm sorry to hear that. Too bad we couldn't all go out one last time to have drinks. Next time." I said.

"Why you asking now?" Mecca said and Vernon shot her a look.

"I'm just saying. We've been here a few weeks now and we haven't been able to hang out. Why now?"

"No reason and since you're just asking. Some of us have jobs and can't sit around twiddling our thumbs waiting on a man to come home."

"You're right. Now I know why you couldn't hang out. You're the one who lets her man whoop on her." Me and Ariel jumped up.

"Don't get mad at me. Shit, it's the reason my man got his hand messed up. He was saving your *working ass*." She folded her arms across her chest.

"I deserve better right?" I was indirectly speaking to Vernon.

"I deserve better than a man pillow talking with his woman about my business. I deserve better than a man who would use and abuse me. I deserve better than a man who would cheat on me too, right?"

"She don't know what she talking about sis. Don't let her get to you." Vernon couldn't take his eyes off me.

"I'm not about to let anyone get to me anymore. Fuck everybody." I stormed upstairs and slammed my door. A few seconds later there was a presence behind me.

"I told her the night it happened because she was at the club too. I never meant for her to bring it up. I apologize Monie." He wrapped his arms around my waist and kissed my neck.

"It doesn't even matter. What happened between us is a distant memory and can never be spoken of so who cares right? You were my first and I appreciated the experience, but you should go." I held back the tears stinging my eyes. I don't even know why I was crying. I guess it's because I thought he was better than telling my business. I understand why he told but damn.

"Armonie." I moved away from him.

"Goodbye Vernon." I sat on the bed with my knees pulled to my chest. I really can't win for losing with men.

"What's going on and why she look upset?" Ariel barged in.

"Nothing. I thanked him for saving me and thinking about certain things brought on some emotions. I'm good sis." Vernon refused to look away.

"VERNON!" Mecca shouted up the steps.

"Have a safe drive." He nodded and walked out backwards.

"And here I thought you'd hook up." Ariel said laying next to me on the bed.

"Time wasn't on our side." Is all I said and dozed off. When I woke up it was midnight. I'm glad this day is over.

Haven

"I didn't expect to see you." This bitch I've been fucking for over a year said.

"Move." I pushed passed her and went straight to the kitchen. She always had beer stocked and I needed a drink.

"The fuck you looking at?" I said to her six-year-old. All the times I've been here, this is the first time I met him.

Yea the bitch had two kids at the age of twenty-four. Maybe that's why her pussy wide open. Whatever the case, I come strictly for the head. I may slide in, here and there but not usually. I still fucks with her though because she cool as hell. I don't always come to get sex from her, and we can have a decent conversation about anything. Outta my top five she's number three.

"You punk. Always coming over drinking up our stuff." He poked is chest out and I wanted to laugh but I couldn't. I asked to see what he'd say. How he even know what it is?

"Nigga you drink beer?"

"Why you questioning me?" I wanted to knock his teeth out.

"Ant, what I tell you about talking to grown-ups like that?" Sharika said coming in the kitchen.

"What I tell you about having different men around us? We don't know him. What if he...?" I yoked his punk ass up.

"Haven please put him down."

"Nah. He tough. Let his ass keep talking." She started crying and I dropped him on the floor.

"I don't care how many niggas your mother has in here, you're gonna respect this one." I pointed to myself.

"Am I clear?" I barked and he jumped.

"Fuck you." I snatched his ass up again, put him on my lap and beat his ass like he was my kid.

"Haven Stop. Oh my God. Please." She tried holding my hand but it didn't do shit. I've never heard a kid speak like that and I fuck with ratchet chicks who have kids too.

"Ahhh. I'm sorry. I'm sorry. Please stop." I pushed him off my lap and stood up.

140

"Yo son disrespectful as shit. Where his father?" I was breathing heavy because I wanted to beat his ass some more.

"He doesn't know about him." She put her head down after saying it silently. I glanced down at the boy.

"What the fuck is wrong with you? That's what's wrong with him. He needs a man in his life." She looked at me.

"Get up!" The little boy hopped off the floor." I sat in the chair and gulped down the beer. I had to in order to calm down.

"Let me talk to your mom." He hauled ass out the kitchen.

"You're the only one I'm..." I put my hand up to stop the lie. I don't even know why she brought it up.

"Sharika we've been messing around for a year and you have a one year old. I know for a fact these kids aren't mine so go head with the lie. Why you not letting your other kids father help you?"

"He in jail and I don't want just any man around them."

"But I'm ok to be around them?" I questioned because she sounded stupid.

"I didn't know you were stopping by and if you noticed, he's never here when you are." I couldn't debate that.

"And besides, everyone knows who you are. I know you're not a pedophile or rapist. You're strong minded and..."

"And you need to tell his daddy." I cut her off because it's the truth.

"Why aren't you telling his dad?"

"He didn't want kids and I did. We had unprotected sex all the time and we knew the consequences but when it happened, he wasn't ready, so he says." She put up air quotes

"You knew them too and now you're raising this kid without his father because you were being sneaky."

"I got tired of the abortions Haven." She fell back in the seat.

"Say what?"

"I loved his father with everything I had, and he claimed to have felt the same. He got me pregnant and begged me to get rid of it because we were young. I agreed and six months later it happened again. We had the same conversation and like a dummy, I had another one. The last time I told him, he left me and said I was getting pregnant on purpose." She let the tears fall down her face. I don't know why but we never discussed her kids' father until today. Maybe it's because they weren't here.

"What?"

"Exactly. I asked him for money to terminate it and he handed it over with no problem. I used the money to go stay with my mother in Texas for a few years so she could help me. Do you know he didn't even look for me? So much for him feeling the same." She shook her head.

"How do you know he wasn't."

"Because I had friends out here and he asked one of them where I went, she told him Texas and he said ok. Not once did he ask for a number, address, nothing. He went on with his life like I never existed." I didn't say a word. Something still sound suspect about her story but I'll listen.

"I only returned to Jersey because of a job." She said and stood to throw the beer bottle away.

143

"A job?"

"Yea. My aunt works over at the post office and she got me right in with benefits and everything. I had a son and no job. I couldn't pass it up."

"Well have you seen his dad?" She shook her head laughing.

"How can I not? He's everywhere I choose not to go."

"I don't understand."

"Ant has a lot of money and power. If I approached him with my son, he may try to take him and I refuse to lose him."

"I thought you said he didn't want kids."

"He didn't at the time, but I follow his new girlfriend on social media and…"

"Why are you following his girl and how do you even know who she is?" I asked because I don't do social media, but I always thought it was dumb of people to follow someone they don't talk to. You see what they're doing and make yourself mad.

"People talk and I still have friends out here who do hang out. Anyway, she posted a picture of the house he brought her, built from the ground up too. Guess who has no problem showing her off?" I can hear hate in her voice. How she mad at the new girl who had nothing to do with his choices all those years ago?

"He's older now Sharika, which means he may be ready to build and start a family."

"I get it but damn."

"Damn, what?" I asked.

"I wanted what he's giving her." *BAM!* There it is. Sharika wants him back. I just shook my head.

"That's what your nosy ass gets for being on her page."

"Yea, I guess. I just hate to see how happy he is when we could've had three kids and whether we were together or not, at least I didn't abort two of them."

"Damn." I felt bad for her because women deal with this a lot.

"She even posted a video of him asking her to move here so guess who put a transfer in to move back to Texas?"

"I don't agree with how he handled the situation, but you need to tell him." I told her honestly because the man deserved to know. Its too many men out here tryna be a father and the woman won't allow it for whatever reason. I feel like she's being selfish because she's mad he didn't want her to have his kids.

"No thanks." She stood.

"I'll be right back and we can do whatever. Let me check on my son real quick." I grabbed her wrist.

"Another time. This shit just blew me." I handed her all the money I had in my pocket and kissed her cheek.

"Haven, I can't accept this."

"Look at it as an apology gift for beating his ass." She started laughing and tried to hand me the money back.

"He needed it and we both know it."

"He did but I'm not his pops." I went to the door and turned around.

"Think about what I said." She nodded and I walked out the door in deep thought. I wish a bitch would keep my kid from me but then again, their situation is crazy. So much for getting my dick sucked. On to the next chick and I hope she don't have no drama.

146

****

"What Haven?" She answered the phone with an attitude.

"Ariel don't be mad at me. You know how we roll. You should've told your cousin before letting him pop shit." I knew she was still mad over the restaurant situation because Armonie told me.

"Haven you'd never let anyone speak to Armonie the way you spoke to me, would you?"

"Hell no." I stopped at the red light.

"Exactly. He's protective of me the same way you are of her. Everyone doesn't need to know how we interact."

"Whatever. Can I stop by or not?" I wasn't tryna hear shit she had to say.

"Bye." She hung up which only infuriated me. I sped over to their house and used my key to enter. I locked the door and walked straight to her room. I passed Armonie's on the way and saw she was knocked out.

"I said no Haven." I closed her door with my foot, walked over to the bed and stood her against the wall.

147

"You do too much and..." I never kiss but slid my tongue in her mouth anyway. I thought she'd push me off but instead lifted her legs around my waist.

I put her down and stripped her outta the small ass pajamas she wore. Standing there naked, Ariel didn't shy away from my gaze. She had total confidence in her body and she should. It was perfect and all hers. No plastic surgery, implants or nothing. 100% all woman and I loved that shit.

"Come to me Haven." She lifted her leg on the nightstand and used her middle and index finger to caress her pearl.

"This is what you want right? We're both here and it's no time like the present." I moved closer and replaced her hand with mine. She began grinding on my two fingers I slipped inside.

"Right there Haven. Mmm. Yea." I pressed my lips on hers and felt her unbuttoning by jeans. She pulled my dick out and rubbed the tip on her clit that was now sticking out.

"I'm about to cum Haven." She gripped my neck tighter, rubbed my shit faster and grinded on my fingers at the same time.

"Oh shit. Oh shit." Her body began to shake and I couldn't hold out. I stuck all ten inches inside her.

"Fuckkkk!" She screamed out and dug her nails in the top of my shoulder.

"Haven. Go slow. You're big as hell."

"This is what you wanted right? Your words."

"Yes. Shit." She started kissing me again and popping up and down. I squeezed her ass and the two of us were now in sync.

"Oh fuck. You feel so good. Shitt." She bit down on my neck and left her face there to stifle the moans.

"You wetting my dick up Ariel." I looked down and it was almost white. She had already cum three times.

"Haven."

"Yea." I was still watching myself go in and out.

"Tell me when you're about to cum."

"Right now." I wasn't lying. Her pussy was wet and gushy the way I liked it.

"Let me down." She patted my shoulders.

"What?"

"Hurry up." I did like she asked and grabbed on the dresser as she devoured me. I had to stare down to make sure I wasn't dreaming. This nigga told everyone she didn't give good head but the way my toes are curling and eyes are rolling, I'd say he's mistaken.

"Cum in my mouth Haven." She licked my balls and swished them in her mouth like candy.

"Yea baby. Here it comes." The way she spoke drove me insane.

"Mmmm. Shit, you taste good Haven. Mmm." She took her time removing all my seeds. My breathing was erratic and no matter how fast I tried to calm down, I couldn't. She had my ass stuck. She kissed up my stomach and chest before pecking my lips.

"Did I clear up the false rumors?" I snatched her by the hair, stuck my tongue in her mouth and a few minutes later we were back at it. We fucked the shit outta each other for the rest of the night.

"I'm out." I said after getting my clothes on.

"Ok. Lock the door." She barely spoke because sleep was overtaking her. I stared down at the woman who sexed me better than any other woman I've been with and realized we could never do it again. She had the ability to get me strung and I'm good. At least I got to sample the pussy and head.

Ariel

"I thought you were leaving." I said to Vernon when I stepped in my parents' house. He passed by my place saying he was leaving town; yet here he is. I've been working nonstop and going to school; I probably would've have known if I came over sooner.

"You rushing us." Mecca snapped.

"Bitch, I will slide your ass across this got damn room if you get smart one more time."

"Yea ok. Vernon you better get your cousin."

"He don't gotta get shit. Ever since he brought you here, all you've done is bitch. No wonder he wanted to leave your ass home." She looked over at my cousin who had a drink in his hand.

"Shut the fuck up Mecca. You stay popping shit." I smirked and moved past her.

"Like I was saying. What you doing here?" He walked away without answering.

"VJ, What the..." He put his index finger up to his mouth telling me to be quiet. He closed the patio door and sparked up a blunt. After he took a pull, he looked at me.

"I don't wanna leave her." I gave him the side eye.

"Well you should've never brought her." I assumed he didn't wanna leave the Mecca bitch in Virginia when he returned.

"Not her stupid ass."

"Then who you talking about? Is your mom staying?" I know how close he is with her.

"Armonie."

"Armonie? My best friend Armonie?" I pointed to myself.

"What other Armonie is it?"

"Be quiet. I'm asking because y'all not even that close." He took another pull.

"I know y'all ain't fuck because she would've told me." He remained quiet as if he were in a zone.

"Has the nigga been by the house?" He stared into the backyard.

153

"Yea. The same day you mentioned leaving he stopped by. I told him she stayed at her parents' house."

"Has he been back?"

"Not that I know of, but I've been working and going to school. We haven't really seen one another." He nodded and a small grin crept on his face.

"Are you feeling her or something? I mean what's the sudden concern?"

"I feel bad because you know what my mom went through."

"Yea." I said and took a few pulls.

"I'm hoping her taking time to herself will allow her to see she deserves better."

"You mean better than you telling Mecca her business." He turned his neck real fast.

"That was an accident man. I beat dude's ass in the bathroom, and she questioned why my hand was fucked up. I wasn't thinking she'd bring it up and throw it in her face." He seemed very apologetic.

"Why do I feel like you low key feeling my friend?"

"I'm gonna move up here with the family because we have people in Virginia to handle things. If it's a problem I can hop a flight."

"You doing a lot for someone who basically just met her."

"I know Monie."

"Yea but y'all weren't close and..."

"Damn cuz. You interrogating the shit outta me. I may as well have Mecca out here." He barked. I noticed how he ignored my statement about him feeling Armonie.

"My bad. I won't bring it up again but know this." I stood to go inside.

"Mecca ain't welcomed at my house again and if you decide to pursue Armonie, DON'T." He lifted his head to look at me.

"She don't need anymore drama in her life right now and the bitch you have is nothing but drama." I swung my body around and left him sitting out there. I loved my cousin but if he's dealing with this bitch, Armonie is off limits.

"Hey daddy." He was in the kitchen rubbing on my mom.

"Guess I'm invisible." She joked.

"Hey ma. I need to talk to daddy tho."

"You ok?" She asked with a concerned look.

"Yea. It's about the new building and stuff." She waved me off because me and my dad could talk for hours about those things.

"Let's go." VJ barked at Mecca and her stupid ass jumped up. Yea Armonie don't need no one else tryna control her. I followed my dad in his office.

"What's up?"

"Ok so, I have a dilemma."

"With who?" He poured himself a drink.

"How you know it's with a who?" I asked.

"Because you mentioned discussing business and now you're saying you have a dilemma. Can't be about no business because the building ain't done." I snickered. My dad could see straight through me like everyone else; which is why I hated lying to Armonie's parents.

156

"Well, there's this guy." His face cringed up. He knows what Eddie said about me and Brayden whooped his ass. It was bad too. Eddie ended up in the hospital. *Oh well.*

"Hear me out." He leaned back in his chair with his hands intertwined on his stomach. You know the way teachers look down on students.

"This guy and I argue every time we see each other. I mean it's gets really bad and he knows how to press all my buttons." I told him.

"Ok."

"Ok so. We were out and he sorta disrespected me." My father sat up quick.

"Not like that, well I guess if you didn't know our relationship you'd assume otherwise." He wasn't saying anything.

"Anyway, he's the one who fought VJ for standing up for me."

"Keep going." He waved his hand in circles to tell me to hurry up.

"Well he says some foul things to me but is it sad that I don't look at it the way others would because we go back and forth all the time. It just happened to be in front of VJ this time."

"Ariel your mother taught you a long time ago never to let a man say what he wants and laugh it off as a joke because he'll think it's ok to do it."

"I do know but he's been around forever and it's how we talk." I rested my head on the seat.

"Do you look at it as being disrespectful?"

"Sometimes but I give it right back to him."

"Why is this a problem? Am I missing something besides you telling me you're gonna make sure he respects you from now on?"

"No it's just Haven's a different breed and..."

"I know damn well this conversation better not involve Haven Banks." I put my head down.

"Ariel. That nigga crazier than your brother and we know he ain't got it all." I started laughing.

"Daddy, he is but now that we've been together intimately..."

"Ariel really? Outta all the men in the world you choose the got damn Reaper?" Yea my dad knew all about him because him and Brayden been friends since kids.

"It just happened."

"Nothing just happens."

"Fine. He had the key Armonie gave him, dropped over one night and neither of us objected to the sexual chemistry that took place." I was trying not to say sex. He may be my father and listen when I speak but the word sex to my father is like poison. He doesn't wanna hear his first daughter is having sex or my younger sister.

"Sounds like its more than just a sexual chemistry." He stood and poured himself another drink.

"Actually no. He's rude, ignorant, arrogant, embarrassing and don't know how to be quiet."

"Then why did you sleep with him?" He turned to me with the cup at his mouth.

"I don't know. I don't regret it but I also don't want him thinking I'm one of his jump offs. So the question I have is, how do I tell him it was a one-time thing?"

"Was it?"

"Yea. We haven't spoken since that night."

"He may already be looking at it the same as you. But if you wanna know, text or call him."

"I guess." He sat next to me.

"You can have this exact conversation with your mom, aunts and whoever else and we're all gonna say the same thing."

"What's that?" He lifted my head to make me face him.

"You're feeling him more than you want to and unsure of where his head is. Since he hasn't contacted you, you're tryna figure out a way to distance yourself because you don't wanna be caught up in his web of women. But let me be the first to tell you." He laid back on the small loveseat and I rested my head on his shoulder.

"If you're feeling him and he's the asshole we all know him to be, make him work for you."

"What you mean?"

"Your brother and his crew probably have a bunch of women they sleep with and share. Make it where he doesn't wanna be with another woman. Make him sweat you."

"Sweat me?" Haven doesn't sweat anyone.

"Don't be like these other chicks out here who see dollar signs and want to be on his arm for the wrong reasons. If he wants to get anymore sexual chemistry from you, he has to prove it's you and only you." I laughed when he didn't use the word sex.

"What if he doesn't?"

"Then no matter how good it was, he isn't worth it." I nodded and stayed put.

My father put a lot of things in perspective for me. I ended up staying for dinner and bringing a plate to Armonie. Imagine my surprise seeing Freddy on the couch. I'm disappointed but not surprised. She's scared for her life, yet all this could be avoided if she mentioned it to her parents.

"Mommy sent you a plate." I told her walking in the kitchen.

"He won't leave." She whispered and looked in the living room to make sure he wasn't coming.

"What?" I said above a whisper.

"He came over unexpectedly to talk. He apologized and I told him to go because it's late and he hasn't moved. I don't even think he went to the bathroom once I said it." We busted out laughing.

"You want me to call VJ over?" She gave me a weird look.

"VJ? I thought he left."

"Nope. He's still here and thinking about moving in the area." I told her.

"Oh." I saw the same stupid grin creep on her face that he had on his.

"Bitch, I know y'all didn't fuck."

"No we didn't because she still holding out. I know the pussy better have me strung out for as long as she got me waiting." I'm glad he didn't hear the beginning of the conversation.

"Freddy, I asked you to leave an hour ago." I guess she wasn't lying.

"You did but it's too many crazy people out here. I'm gonna stay the night." He walked out. I went to say something and she stopped me.

"I don't want no problems. Can I stay in your room?" She looked petrified.

"Armonie you can't live like this. We can't live like this."

"I know and we'll get the locks changed tomorrow. Fuck it. Let's move." I asked if she was sure because I've been tryna get outta here, but she loved this place.

"We can stay in one of the condos my dad owns."

"The new ones?" She questioned.

"Yup. And bitch we not done discussing my cousin." She sucked her teeth and ran up the steps. I'm gonna leave it alone for now but she's gonna tell me something.

Haven

"Tha fuck you doing down here?" I barked at my cousins' man and he jumped outta his sleep.

"Armonie got an attitude and stayed in the room with Ariel." I stared at him. The shit sound suspect as fuck.

"Shit sound crazy." I said to see if he'd tell me why she really made him stay down here.

"Yea. You know how she do."

"I do. Now bounce nigga." He looked at me.

"You heard what the fuck I said. Bounce motherfucker." He took his time putting on his sneakers and I told myself to give him a minute but something in me said he was doing the shit on purpose. I remained calm because what I'm here for, I honestly don't need Armonie waking up. I walked over and opened the door for him.

"Is there a reason you making me leave?"

"Not really. I just don't want you here when I am." I shrugged and watched him slowly walk to the door.

"Can I say bye to her?"

"Nigga if she got yo ass on the couch then she ain't tryna hear you say shit."

"A'ight man relax. No need to..." I slammed the door in his face and made a mental note to monitor him.

I locked the door and went up the steps to find my cousin and Ariel asleep in the room. Of course I'm aggravated because I wanted to fuck. I had to figure out a way to get Ariel out the bed without waking Armonie. I could just tap her on the arm but being the dick I am, I snatched the covers off and pulled her to her feet.

"What the fuck?"

"I'ma need you to brush your teeth before I throw up." I spoke as quietly as I could. Armonie tossed and turned for a second and then I heard light snoring.

"Haven why..."

"Ah..." I stopped her and pointed to the bathroom. She stormed in there and I heard the water cut on. Instead of waiting, I went in the guest bedroom and noticed a few things boxed up. What the hell is that about? I sat on the bed and took my sneakers and clothes off.

"What are you doing here Haven and..." I closed the door and pinned her against it. I wasn't about to answer a hundred questions.

"No Haven. You are not about to use me for sex." She moaned out while I kissed and sucked on her neck.

"I'm not using you for shit. I'm gonna continue fucking you." I lifted the shirt over her head and helped her step outta the shorts. Clearly, she want it because she's not stopping me.

"No more sex Haven. Shit yes. Don't stop baby." Is all I heard as I bent down, inserted two fingers and clamped down on her clit. I'm not into eating bitch's pussy unless she mine but I know Ariel ain't no ho regardless of what I say. She's a homebody like Armonie and goes out once in a while.

"I'm cumming Haven." She grabbed onto my head and let me taste her sweetness. I didn't get a chance to do it the last time.

"No more sex huh?" I lifted her legs in the crook of my arms and rammed in. I wasn't tryna hurt her but she needs to know I'm not leaving.

"I ain't gonna lie Ariel. You got some of the best pussy I ever had and that's including my ex. Shit." I went in circles, pulled out and plunged back in. Ariel's eyes were rolling, and the sound of her juices took over the whole room.

"Haven."

"What up?" I stopped, grabbed her hands and flipped her over.

"Don't stop baby." She started throwing her ass back and that's all it took. We went at it until we both tapped out.

"Haven I'm not tryna trap you or give you an ultimatum." I was putting my sneakers on. I didn't want my cousin seeing me here.

"Go head."

"I meant what I said about using me for sex. If we're not a couple, then no more fucking."

"A couple?" I turned around.

"I'm not saying I wanna be your girl. I'm saying I'm a good woman and should be respected. How am I gonna find a good man if I'm sleeping with you?" I stood.

"You're not."

167

"Excuse me!" I shocked myself saying it to her.

"Love don't live here anymore Ariel." I pointed to the spot in my chest where my heart would be. Juicy did a number on me, so I didn't want a girl.

"I get what you saying. But if another nigga get in between these motherfucking thighs, I'll hang you upside down and gut your insides out."

"HAVEN!"

"You heard what the fuck I said." She jumped off the bed and I had to contain myself watching her breasts bounce up and down due to her still being naked.

"You don't get to sleep with other women and tell me to close my legs. You are not my man and..." I moved closer and she backed up against the wall.

"I can do what I want, and you got one time to let me hear you dipped out." I moved the messy hair out her face.

"You belong to me and only me." Ariel was definitely beautiful and worth more than I could give her. However, being selfish, I'm not tryna hear it.

"And who do you belong to?"

"Nobody but I'll never allow a bitch to approach you. You'll never hear about anything I do in the streets and I'll make sure you're always satisfied."

"This isn't right Haven."

"You shouldn't have given me any."

"That's bullshit. You fuck bitches all the time."

"You're not a bitch and I definitely don't just fuck you and we both know it." She couldn't say shit. Both nights we slept together our connection was deep. We weren't only exploring each other but making sure we left a mark and it's exactly what we did.

"Take heed to my warning Ariel. I'd hate to end you, but I will." I kissed her forehead and walked out. She can act crazy if she wants, she know the Reaper don't discriminate.

****

"What's up with your cousin?" I asked Brayden while we sat in the truck waiting for this nigga to come out.

Ever since I left Armonie's house a few nights ago, I've been looking into her man. He's not a bad guy that I know of but something ain't right. I've never known my cousin to make him sleep on the couch and if he's the one who broke her virginity, why wouldn't he be in bed with her tryna fuck? Not that I wanna hear about her in bed with a man and I'm not even sure she lost her virginity but something's up.

"Which one?" He passed me the blunt.

"The one I had the boys fight."

"Nigga how you gonna have him jumped when he helped your cousin?" Brayden is the only nigga I fuck with who could question me about anything besides my family.

"Yo! He was whooping Jerome ass. I couldn't let him go out like that. I swear your cousin was about to kill him."

"Yea. VJ know all different types of fighting techniques. He only gets that bad if someone pissed him off."

"It makes me wonder if he's the one who beat this punk up in the bathroom." Freddy stepped out the house checking his surroundings before getting in his car. Who he looking for?

"He's the one." I looked at him.

"Why he fight him?"

"Look Haven. You my boy but that's some shit you need to discuss with Freddy and Armonie." When he said that my antennas went up again.

"That's what your cousin said at the restaurant."

"Definitely look into it. Let's go." He put the blunt out and pulled behind Freddy. I couldn't help but think about what he said. I'm gonna get it outta Ariel because Armonie scary ass ain't gonna say shit.

We drove two cars behind him and parked down the street when he pulled up to his mother's house. There were mad people outside like it was a party. Some were posted on the porch drinking, others in front of cars and chicks twerking their dirty ass in the street.

"Ain't that your cousin?" He pointed to Armonie who stood there with Stormy and Ariel.

"Yup." I sent a message to Ariel's phone.

Me: *If you give a nigga your phone number or even conversation, I'm gonna ram my dick in your ass.* I saw her look down and then searched the area.

171

Me: *Don't worry about if I'm there or not, just know I mean it.*

Ariel: *Fuck you punk. You don't scare me.* I noticed some guy walk over with Freddy and stand in her face. She shook her head no and walked behind Armonie and Stormy. The dude was staring at her ass and it aggravated me.

Me: *That's what I thought.*

Ariel: *Whatever. He was ugly, that's the only reason why I didn't entertain him.*

Me: *Yea ok. You know what it is.* I put my phone away and watched the awkward interaction between Armonie and Freddy. It seemed as if she was forcing herself to be there.

"My sister got yo ass stuck." Brayden said laughing. He knew we took it there but this is the first time we talked about it since.

"Fuck you."

"I'm just saying. We here for your cousin and you watching Ariel."

"I'm watching my cousin too." I stared at Freddy pull Armonie in front of him and felt a tad bit better.

172

"We getting out?" Brayden asked getting his gun ready. One would think he followed in his pops footsteps by running the buildings he owned but not him. He's almost as crazy as me.

"Nah." I reached in my pocket to grab the phone I just put away and laughed at the text.

Ariel: *Since I can only fuck you, I better have you in my bed no later than 1 or I promise to come looking for you. I'm gonna act the fuck up too. Try me.*

Me: *You ain't running shit.*

Ariel: *You heard what the fuck I said.*

"Damn nigga. Let me get you home before she wild out."

"Let me find out you reading my text."

"Get a privacy screen punk." He joked and pulled off.

Armonie

"If you even think about opening your mouth to my mom, I'll break your jaw." Freddy whispered in my ear when we walked on the porch. I didn't wanna come and had his mom not asked, I wouldn't have.

I know people may be calling me stupid and dumb and you're right. I'm scared to tell my family because they'll kill him. I shouldn't care but I do. Then, I'm scared he'll kill me if I don't want him. Why does being in a relationship have to be so hard? There's no way he's in love if threatening me is the only way to keep me around.

"Freddy stop with the threats ok? I'm tired of it." I stepped away from him and into the house. I hated being around this many people because someone is bound to fight, tell somebody's business and drink until they pass out; yet, here I am.

"Armonieeeee." His mother always extended my name when she saw me.

"Hi, Mrs. Graham. How are you?" We embraced one another for a few seconds.

"Hey Ariel and is this the pastor's daughter?" She pointed to Stormy.

"Yes I am. How are you?" Stormy spoke in a polite manner.

"I'm good. Is your father happy?" Mrs. Graham said throwing all of us off.

"Excuse me. I'm not sure I understand what you're asking." We were all confused.

"I'm just saying, he is fine as hell and whew!" She fanned herself.

"Yes, my dad is happily married." We all laughed.

"Girl, they don't make them as fine as your dad. Look at what God sent me." She pointed to her husband and we all busted out laughing. He was drunk as hell and talking shit at the table. There was a card game going on and it's clear he was losing.

"I'll let him know you find him attractive."

"That's ok. Don't nobody need your crazy ass mother tryna fight."

"You already know." Stormy told her and shared another laugh. It was funny tho.

"Let me talk to you for a minute." She told the girls we'd be right back. The bedroom door closed, and I sat on the old-fashioned recliner in the room. Old people kept everything.

"What's going on with you and my son?"

"I don't know what you mean." She sat on the windowsill in front of me.

"You barely call anymore and after seeing you in the hospital the last time, I have to ask, is it worth it?" I laid my head back on the chair.

"We used to be so happy and when I wouldn't give him sex, things changed. He cheated and the abuse started..."

"Abuse? He told me some guy from outta town did that to you and he tried to beat him up and got jumped." I chuckled because Vernon did a number on him.

"Actually, your son has been beating on me for almost a year now. Believe it or not he warned me not to mention it today." She shook her head.

"I remember when his father used to beat on me. Boy, did I love that man." She shook her head.

"And you stayed?"

"Not at first. You see, I took a hell of a lotta of beatings. Broken bones, jaw, nose and the emotional abuse was even worse. Four long years of being scared to leave, scared for my life and scared to be on my own."

"What did you do?" She smiled.

"One night he was asleep, and I had, had enough. I poured gasoline on his legs, set them on fire and stood in front of him with a fire extinguisher. He begged and pleaded for me to put it out and I wouldn't until he swore, he'd never hit me again."

"Oh my God." I covered my mouth.

"Chile please. It worked for sure and I hadn't had a problem since."

"What did the hospital say? You didn't go to jail."

177

"He told them the gasoline from the lawn mower spilled on him and he was smoking."

"And they believed him?"

"Yup. They could care less if he killed himself. Another black man they don't have to worry about."

"Is that why he doesn't wear shorts?"

"You got it. His legs are fucked up." We both laughed.

"Honey, if you're not strong enough to handle the abuse, then leave." *Did this woman say if I can't handle it? Who's strong enough for that?* She obviously wasn't because she tried to burn him alive.

"I don't wanna die and I don't want my family to kill him so I'm trying to figure it out." She knew who my family was just like everyone else.

"I'd rather you leave and move on. I don't wanna bury my son." She patted my shoulder and left the room. I wish it were that easy. I went to leave the room and his sister blocked me in.

"If anything happens to my brother for beating your ass were gonna have a problem." She had her arms folded.

"Latifa you don't scare me. I suggest you move the fuck on." I pushed her out the way.

"Put your hands on her and I'll break your wrist." I turned to see VJ standing there with two other guys.

"VJ fuck her. She's tryna get my brother killed." Latifa yelled.

"He shouldn't be putting his hands on her." He lifted the beer to drink.

"You know her?"

"The fact you're asking if I know her and not dealing with your brother beating on her, is a problem."

"But she…"

"Get the fuck out my face Latifa." She caught an attitude.

"I'm saying. Are you still staying the night?" I folded my arms and waited for him to answer.

"My girl downstairs and you asking me some dumb shit. You desperate as fuck yo. Beat it." He waved her off and she stormed away.

"Can y'all give us a minute?" The two dudes moved down the hall. The house wasn't huge, but the upstairs did have a small hallway.

"You good?" He asked and took another sip.

"I'm fine. What are you doing here and are you sleeping with her too?" He smiled and backed me against the wall.

"The only woman I've slept with since being here is you and it's gonna stay that way." He placed a kiss on my neck.

"I miss you Monie." His index finger lifted my chin. He slid his tongue in my mouth and had we been elsewhere, we'd probably be naked.

"I want you in my bed tonight or I can come to you." He wiped his bottom lip.

"VJ you have a girl and I'm not playing second to no one."

"No disrespect but I'm doing the same thing because yo nigga downstairs."

"Touché. The difference is we're not sleeping together and never will." I was serious. Freddy is too crazy and I know if we slept together it would get worse.

"You haven't slept with him?" He seemed confused.

"Hell no! If we slept together I'd have more problems."

"Oh." Is all he said which let me know he's sleeping with Mecca.

"You thought because you were my first, I'd just go and fuck him?" I was offended.

"I didn't say that and I'm glad you didn't." He stared at me.

"I should go." He didn't move.

"Why didn't we meet, or should I say, mess around years ago?" I smiled and moved outta his embrace.

"It wasn't meant to be." I excused myself walking past the other guys.

"Where the fuck you been?" Freddy grabbed my arm when I hit the bottom step.

"Get off." I tried to get outta his grip.

"You think I'm ok with other niggas in your face?"

181

"What are you talking about?" I wonder if he saw me and VJ kissing?

"Latifa told me how you were in some guys face. How you at my mom's house acting like a ho?"

"That's enough Freddy. Let her go." His mom shouted and he pushed me on the ground.

BAM! I looked up and VJ knocked him out.

"You ok?" He reached out to help me.

"Yea. I'm just gonna leave."

"Bye bitch. Take your crippled ass the fuck outta here." Latifa shouted and VJ stared at me. People knew about my leg, but no one ever mentioned it. I'm sure she couldn't wait to shout it since VJ told her to beat it so he could speak to me in private.

The night VJ and I shared a bed, I had shoes on so he couldn't tell, and he carried me all over the room, so he wasn't able to see then either. When I say it's hard to notice, it really is. Walking hurts sometimes without shoes which is why I'm always in slippers at my house. You can tell when I'm barefoot though.

"Crippled?" Mecca questioned just as Ariel and Stormy came in the house laughing. They stopped after seeing my face.

"Yup. The bitch got two different legs. One is bigger than the other. Pay attention and you'll see. I don't know why my brother wanted to be with you. Your baby would probably be deformed if y'all had kids."

"Wow! VJ you didn't tell me she's disabled." Mecca said and Ariel jumped on her. I walked over to Latifa and did the same. I could hear Stormy telling every chick in there to stay put.

BOOM! A gun went off.

"That's enough." I heard and stood there with tears falling down my face. I don't know if it were because she shouted it out or I was embarrassed she said it in front of VJ.

"Go home Ariel and Monie." VJ barked. Ariel started to say something and stopped when she saw his face.

"If any motherfucker in here disrespect Armonie again I'm knocking you the fuck out." Nobody said a word as we

183

walked out. Did these people know him because no one said a word?

"I'm done Ariel. I can't do this anymore." I cried going to the car.

"You want me to call your brother?"

"No. I'm gonna stay at the hotel tonight and move in with my parents. When you get the new place, I'll move in with you but right now I need some peace."

We drove in silence to drop Stormy off. She gave me a hug and promised to call tomorrow. Once Ariel pulled into the hotel, she walked in with me, stayed for about an hour and left. I stayed on the phone with her until she made it to the house.

"It's not one o clock but you better had been here?" Ariel spoke to someone.

"Who is that?" I asked and started the jacuzzi.

"None of your business. Call me in the morning. Mmmm. You taste like weed." The guy never said a word.

"Bitch who is that?"

"Bye Armonie." The phone hung up. I tossed mine on the bed and headed to the bathroom.

BOOM! BOOM! BOOM! BOOM! My heart started beating fast. I had no one here and my energy is non existent. I peeped through the small window and blew my breath. Why is he here?

Vernon

"Get up." I barked at Mecca on the floor. I wasn't even mad my cousin beat her ass because she deserved it.

"VJ why you let her fight me?" Did she really just ask me that?

"I told you to stop fucking with her." I pushed her out the front door. It's bad enough her eye was swollen shut and her nose looked broke. I didn't need anymore people seeing her.

"VJ are you coming back?" Mecca stopped. Latifa just got her ass beat and still being smart.

"Coming back for what?"

"Bitch to fuck. What you think?" Mecca went towards her.

"How the fuck both of y'all get yo ass beat and still tryna fight? Y'all look dumb as hell." I left Mecca standing there and went to my car. My boy sat in the back while she sat in the front.

"VJ I'm tired of your cousin and her bitch ass friend. They always getting smart and..." I stopped her right there.

"Stop playing victim and take responsibility for the petty shit you say and do." Her mouth dropped.

"You had no business getting in the mess with Latifa. Then you get smart with Ariel and for what? You know what? I'm not tryna deal with this." I pulled off and drove her straight to the condo.

"I'm dropping him off and I might be back." I stepped out the car and unlocked the door.

"I know you're not going to that dirty woman."

"Hell no I'm not. Are you crazy?" I barked and walked back to the car.

"What time you coming home?"

"I don't know. Lock up." I pulled out the driveway.

"I love you VJ." I heard her because the window was down. I hit her with the peace sign and kept it moving.

"Yo! That was wild. Shorty ok?" My boy Mycah asked. He knew how I felt about Mecca and also how I started feeling Monie. Besides Brayden, he's my best friend. We grew up together in Virginia and been rocking with each other ever since.

"She has a room at the hotel you staying at. I'm gonna go check on her." He laughed.

"Yea a'ight. You bout to fuck." We started laughing.

"I'll see you later." I went in the opposite direction of where he was going. I remembered the room in an area all by itself. It made me wonder how she got it. I banged on the door and threw my tongue down her throat when she opened it.

"VJ what are you doing here?" She pushed me away.

"I had to check on you."

"I'm fine. You can go." I closed the door with my foot, locked it and carried her in the bathroom.

"Were you waiting for me?" I pointed to the water in the jacuzzi.

"No. I just wanted to relax."

"Good because I need to do the same." I stripped out my clothes, removed hers and helped her in. I sat down and mounted her on top.

"Sssss." I could see pain etched on her face.

"You ok?" I held her waist.

"I'm still getting used to having sex. It's gonna take me a minute to adjust that's all." I watched as she got comfortable and bit my lip when she started grinding in circles.

"You got it ma." I lifted her hips and slammed her down.

"I see why he don't want no one to have this and he hasn't even had it. Shit, I know how you feel and I don't want anyone to know." I placed my finger on her clit and enjoyed the facial expressions she made as her orgasm started building.

"Did you miss me Monie?"

"Yesss. I missed you a lot." I pulled her neck close to my face for a kiss and continued circling her pearl.

"Mmmm." She moaned in my mouth as the first one erupted.

"You look sexy cumming." I told her and made her do it again. We ended up having sex in the jacuzzi, the floor and I put her back on the table to eat her pussy. The glistening of her pussy under the light had me amazed. No wonder doctors be in it.

"Why did she call you crippled?" I asked when we finished. She was laying on my chest and I felt her body tense up.

"Don't be embarrassed Monie. It's not gonna stop me from coming to see you or look at you in a different light." She blew her breath

"I'm a pre mature baby and the doctors think my short leg is the outcome of it."

"Oh. But you can't tell." You really couldn't.

"You can when I'm barefoot. I mean it's not really bad but sometimes it hurts if I walk without a shoe too long. It's like each step puts more weight on the other leg."

"Why didn't I notice?"

"Ugh because your head and body has been in between my legs. And why would you think to pay attention, when you didn't know about it?"

"True." We laughed.

"She only said it to hurt me because everyone knows how sensitive I am about it." I pulled her body on mine.

"Well it don't bother me and it doesn't interfere with how you fuck, which is real good by the way. I taught you well." I moved her hair back.

"You did but you only taught me how to please you." I used my elbows to lift up and stared down at her.

"And I'm the only one you need to please."

"Whatever."

"I mean it Monie."

"VJ, I don't wanna argue. You made sure I had an amazing night and I wanna remain happy."

"Yea a'ight. Don't play with me."

"You're just saying that because you were my first. I know damn well you've experienced women way better than me."

"I would never compare you to anyone. You're one of a kind Armonie and that's some real shit."

"One of a kind?" She asked and rested her chin on my stomach.

"Something about you is drawing me closer and keeping me near. When you're not around me, I wanna know where you are and if you're safe. Shit, I don't even worry about Mecca, the way I worry about you." She sat up and I could feel her juices sliding out and onto my stomach.

"Is it because I remind you of what your mom went through?"

"Yes, I see my mom in you but I don't know everything you've been through. But I also love making love to you. The way you moan my name and cum has me mesmerized every time."

"Are you strung out?" I chuckled.

"Nah but I love being inside you and I don't want anyone else to feel what I feel. To experience any sexual positions with you or see the facial expressions you make when you cum. I wanna be the only man to have those visions."

"But we both have someone and…"

"And that's where our problem is." I sat all the way up and kissed her in a tender way. Not to rough and not to gentle, just enough to get us aroused again.

"What are we gonna do because right now I'm your side chick and you're my side nigga." I laughed.

"I'll figure it out soon but right now, let's continue making each other happy even if it's only while we're here."

"Ok. Can I do this?" She moved down slowly and had me gripping the sheets and damn near moaning her name. Mecca can suck dick too but this virgin or should I say ex-virgin is about to have my ass in love with the things she's learned to do.

When she finished, I laid there with her in my arms. How could she and I feel right? Whatever is going on, I don't want it to end but I know it will unless we both leave who we're with.

****

"You stayed out all night and half the morning. Then you roll up in here jumping straight in the shower." Mecca whined.

"If I stayed out all night and came in looking the same, explain why I wouldn't shower?" She didn't say a word.

"Exactly! Get dressed." She sucked her teeth.

"For what? My face is messed up and I'm not going anywhere."

"A'ight. Sit in the house all day but I'm not." I turned the shower on and enjoyed the hot water beating down on me.

Monie and I slept well last night together. I had plans on being gone before she woke up but I couldn't leave her. We ended up having sex most of the morning and she showed me her legs. Like she said, you can barely tell but when she has no shoes on there is a difference in the walk. It didn't bother me either way because the sex is great. I've never been with a virgin and who knew she'd catch on quick and fuck me well?

I felt Mecca behind me and rushed to get out. My body is drained, and it wouldn't be fair to sleep with her knowing I've been with someone else. I could do it but keeping the memories from last night and this morning seem better. I don't know what Monie did or how she got me to be her protector but as of right now, I'm not going nowhere. What turned into a week of being here, has lasted a lot longer.

"You fucked her last night?" Mecca questioned when I stepped out the shower.

"Fucked who?" I grabbed the towel and began drying off. She was still in the shower talking.

"I don't know. I do know you've never turned me down for sex. So either you fucked her or allowed her to suck you off." I wrapped the towel around my waist.

"Did you ever think a nigga gets tired of his bitch talking shit everywhere they go? Tired of having to shut motherfuckers down because you can't keep your mouth shut? Tired of fucking his girl with two condoms because he can't trust her enough not to?"

"VJ you know I'm not with anyone else because someone would've told you."

"Is that right?" I stared at her washing up. She didn't even wanna look at me.

"How long you been dealing with Raheem?" I never waited for an answer and stepped out to get dressed. When my boy arrived, he informed me of her dealing with some bum ass dude in Virginia. Its all good though because what goes around comes around. I no longer felt bad for sleeping with Armonie.

"Ok fine." She shut the shower off and came in the room dripping wet. I tossed a towel at her because I don't need my dick reacting.

"I was texting him a few months ago because you were always working, and I was lonely."

"Working Mecca, not fucking some bitch or bitches." I was only back and forth to Maryland and the other condos. You would think I went outta the country, but when I did, she was with me.

"Keep going." I wanted to see how far she really went with him.

"We met up a few times for lunch but never slept together." "Did you kiss him?" She put her head down.

"A'ight. Cool." I didn't say another word.

"VJ we both know you're not faithful." I chuckled because before Monie, I was.

"You know the sad part about this situation is, I didn't wanna bring you but you begged and my mom said why not? I get you here, fuck you damn near every night, take you out to parties with me and you're still not satisfied. If you feel lonely then why not leave?" She sat on the bed crying. I finished getting my things to leave.

196

"Truth be told, Mycah and some of the other guys clowned me all the time for not cheating on you." She lifted her head. I put my belt on and finished what I had to say.

"Yea bitches approached me but just like I told Latifa; I have a girl and I hate a desperate bitch. I never disrespected you and gave you whatever you wanted. Yet; something was missing, and I can't tell you what because I thought I was doing everything right."

"You were VJ. I was just listening to my friends." She cried.

"The same friends who tried to fuck me on the side? The same ones who let you get so drunk, you drive home, and get into an accident. Those same bitches who don't give a fuck about you?" Now she was hysterical.

"Have your stuff packed and ready by the time I get back. We're leaving." I left her on the bed looking like the fool she is.

I wasn't the perfect man, but I was good to her and like I said, before Monie I never cheated on her. Bitches can talk shit about the freaky things they can do and how much better they are then my girl, but I'm not a weak nigga. A fat ass is nice and the pussy may be good but it's not worth the hard work I put in my relationship. Maybe coming here was a sign to get rid of her.

Stormy

"What Curtis?" I opened the door for my ex, who I didn't invite here.

"Can't we talk about this?" He stepped in and stood there.

"Talk about what? When I wanted to talk or work on this relationship you were too busy. Now you see I'm not sitting at home waiting, you're willing to try." I had my arms across my chest.

"I'm sorry." He closed the door and grabbed my waist from behind.

"Let go." I removed his arms and turned around.

"So that's it? You're but even going to try with me?" Why he mad?

"For what Curtis? Huh? You to do it to me again and have me out here looking like a fool? Why would I do that?"

"We been together for a long time and..."

"And it's over. Please go." I re opened the door and he stood there with a smirk on his face.

"Fuck that. I'm not going anywhere until..."

"Until what?" Christian emerged from the bedroom in just his sweats and wife beater. I had to bite down on my lip because he was so damn sexy to me.

"Hold on. You fucking the deacon?" I laughed. Curtis knew who Christian was because in the beginning I had him attending church services with me

"What she does is none on your business, is it?" Christian walked up on him and Curtis looked scared as hell. Everyone knew who his family was and if I weren't cool with them, I'd be nervous too.

"Umm. No, I was just..."

"You were just leaving." Christian pushed him towards the door.

"This is not over. I'm coming back for what's mine."

BAM! Christian punched him so hard he fell into the outside wall. I know his family is ruthless and he has some hood in him but this right here, turned me all the way on.

"You're the second person who allowed my Deacon status to fool them. Don't let it happen again."

"Yooo! The Deacon just hit me. Did you see that?" My neighbor from church stood in the hallway

"I didn't see a thing son." Her back was turned but I'm sure she saw him hit the wall.

"What? Old lady you were right there." Curtis yelled and pissed Mrs. Sands off.

"I can't see without my glasses honey. But don't ever call me an old lady again." She wasn't lying. Mrs. Sands had glaucoma and recently a cataract or something. I had to help her bring things in a few times.

"Fuck you bitch." Mrs. Sands gasped and held her chest. Christian was so angry I had to hold him back.

"Ahhhhh!" Curtis screamed as Mrs. Sands maced him.

"Close your door Stormy before the smell comes in." I did like she asked and stared through the peephole. She was hitting Curtis with her umbrella and purse hard as hell.

"Stormy?" Christian called and I turned around to see him ass naked.

Ever since we've been together, he's turned into another person. He's happier, carefree and even the congregation is happy to know he's divorcing Elaina. A few of the women tried to hook him up with their daughters, and he kindly turned them down. He better had because I don't plan on letting him go no time soon. No one knew about us yet and we wanted to keep it that way until after the divorce.

"Is all that for me?" He slowly stroked himself.

"Depends on if you get naked with me." I moved towards him and took my shirt and booty shorts off.

"You've been turning me out sexy." He watched me get on my knees to please him.

"You don't like it?" I asked and licked the tip.

"I love it. I didn't know making love to a woman could be this good. Mmm." He bit down on his lip when I took him in.

"I know now what your father meant when he said a woman can bring you to your knees sexually if she's really good. Got damn Stormy." I stroked him faster and soon after he came down my throat.

"Let me do some things to you." He laid me down on the floor and I swear, I screamed I loved him.

****

"Great service pastor." I was standing next to my father when the woman spoke. I looked up and it was the same lady in Freddy's house.

"Thanks Mrs. Graham. How's that husband of yours?" He asked and she rolled her eyes.

"Good. Still a loser but we took our vows." My dad chuckled.

"I'm glad you're staying together." Her eyes roamed my father's body.

"It's best you move on." My mother whispered in her ear from behind. Mrs. Graham had no idea she was standing there.

It's no secret a lot of the women have a crush on my dad. However; Serena Burns don't play any games when it comes to him. Everyone loved and respected her but you always had some who'd try their luck.

I can't tell you over the last five years from what I remember, how many times my mother and aunt Tanisha had to fight women or do unheard of things. My uncle Gary isn't into church like my parents, but aunt Tanisha makes him come on Sunday's. Sometimes I think it's the only reason these women attend.

"Oh. Mrs. Burns, how are you?"

"I'm doing good. Can't wait to get home and make love to my husband. What about you?" Mrs. Graham turned her face up and walked away.

"I want it freaky Serena." My dad whispered in her ear, but I heard.

"Really?"

"What? I told your mother when she approaches a woman over me, they come with consequences."

"Good consequences tho." He pecked her lips.

"Bye." I went to walk away but she grabbed my hand.

"Let's talk." She swooped her arm in mine and we stepped out the room. My father was still speaking to everyone like he did every Sunday. Christian walked past, spoke to my mom and smiled at me. We've been staying with one another every night. I loved waking up to him and he said, he felt the same.

"Soooooo." My mom said closing my father's office door. She had her own office but she's hardly ever in there.

"So, what?"

"Don't play with me little girl. You and Christian." She sat down in the chair.

"We're just having fun."

"He's still married Stormy." She said and reclined the chair back.

"I've seen the separation papers and the divorce lawyer served her two weeks ago."

"How long you been sleeping together?" I put my head down. It hasn't been that long but I knew where she was going with it.

"Look, I don't like the heffa myself and you two have grown up together. Y'all know everything about the other so I don't doubt the feelings are there but Stormy, you know the family he comes from."

"I do know and they all love me."

"But will he when he finds out what you're dealing with? Have you told him?" I put my head down.

"Stormy, you can't start a relationship off holding secrets."

"I know but why even bring it up? Its obviously not affecting him." I shrugged my shoulders.

"I understand but if he finds out, its going to be a strain on what you two are trying to build." I didn't say anything.

"Stormy you know I love Christian and I would love to see you two grow but honey, you need to tell him."

"I will mom, just not right now. Let his divorce go through and right before we tell the world about us, I'll tell him." She shook her head.

"You're grown Stormy so I can't make you. I hope it doesn't come back to bite you in the ass." I laid down on my father's loveseat and thought about what she was asking me to do. Could I tell him?

"Stormy do you have anyone's phone number in Christian's family?" My dad barged in.

"Yea. I can call Armonie. Is everything ok?"

"Call and tell her the cops just arrested Christian."

"What?" I hopped up and ran out the door only to see them putting him in the police car. I grabbed my phone and called Armonie.

"Mmmm, hold on." I heard a slight moan out her mouth and tried to contain my laughter. I knew about the affair her and VJ were having. I'm the only one because she didn't want anyone judging her and Ariel would definitely be mad. She hated Freddy but she wouldn't want her cousin with Armonie until she was fully broken up with him.

He's been here for the last few months now and every week, he'd leave for the day and come right back. This time he was leaving, he wasn't returning for a while but who really knows? He appeared to have feelings for Armonie, so I don't know. He said for these last few days, he wanted to spend every moment he could with her.

"ARMONIE!" I shouted.

"Sorry Stormy. VJ won't let me get up." She started laughing.

"Ok look. I need you to call your uncle Wolf. Christian got arrested…" I said in one breath.

"WHAT?" She yelled in the phone.

"I'm going down to the station now."

"Ok, I'm calling my family." She hung up and I grab

my things to go down and see what the hell is going on.

Christian

"I'm not having an affair Elaina because we're not together, so if I am sleeping with someone its none of your business." I told her outside the church. I saw her when she walked in with her mother. I hadn't spoken to her since she cursed me out over the lawyer sending her the divorce papers. She can be in denial about what's going on all she wants, but I'm not.

"Christian, you're sleeping with someone and its not me. Until the judge signs off you're still married."

"She's right Christian. You're the deacon and committing adultery." Her mom chimed in with a grin on her face.

"I am a deacon who filed separation papers; therefore, allowing me to do what I want without considering it adultery. Second, why are you even entertaining your daughter's nonsense. You've been through three husbands so you should know the ropes by now." She seemed offended.

"Christian that was very rude." Elaina said and expected me to apologize. I moved closer to her.

"What's rude is you and your ignorant mother thinking its ok to come here with this nonsense and on a Sunday. Don't you have packing to do?" I asked regarding the house she didn't want to place her name on the deed to. I offered it to her, as well as mentioning signing it over but she refused it.

"That's our house and I'm taking it and everything else in the divorce." I laughed.

"Did you forget you refused to sign the paperwork because your mama said what happened if I didn't want to pay anymore? You would be responsible for the mortgage." Her mouth dropped.

"Feel free to keep the cars because my new woman would never drive anything you were in. As far as taking my money, you signed a prenup too." I shrugged my shoulders.

"So it is someone else?" I saw her eyes getting watery."

"What do you want from me Elaina? Huh? You used to be the best wife ever and then you let your mother get in your ear. You didn't wanna cook, clean or even have sex anymore.

You can't stand my family so why is this divorce hard on you? I'm giving you and out, take it." I turned and saw the pastor coming in my direction. His eyes grew big and before I could turn around, I felt something hit the back of my head.

"What the…?" I swung my body around and noticed a baseball on the ground.

"CHRISTIAN?" I heard the pastor calling my name but it was too late. I already had my hands around Elaina's neck.

"Your best bet is to never come around me again because I will kill you." I tossed her to the side where the bushes were and watched her head hit the side of the church.

"OH MY GOD!" Her mom yelled.

"Get the fuck outta here." I was so mad, they had me cursing.

"911. Yes, I have an emergency and please send the cops. My daughters husband tried to kill her." Her mom spoke in the phone. I leaned against the wall with my leg up and waited for the police.

When they got there, she was being dramatic, and I knew they were going to arrest me. I hope they have life insurance because the Reaper is not going to take this well.

****

"Mr. Banks, I'm sorry about the situation and we're going to handle it quickly." The lawyer said in the captain's office.

"I shouldn't have put my hands on her. My mother taught me better than that." I had my head in my hands thinking about the way I held Elaina in the air. Yes, she deserved it but I've never laid hands on her.

"It was a reaction from her attacking you with a baseball." The captain said and showed me a video Pastor Burns must've sent him. He had cameras everywhere and I'm glad he did.

"Ok. You are getting out on your own recognizance and a court date will be sent in the mail. On the way out, grab the restraining order I had put in place." I went to speak and he stopped me.

"Its to protect you because she's gonna run with this and since she's not on the deed, there's no need for her to return to the house." I nodded and stood.

"This is crazy." I was more upset with myself for allowing Elaina to take me there.

"Its all going to work out in your favor; especially when the judge sees the video. Don't worry Christian." The lawyer said and patted my shoulder on the way out the door.

I walked in the lobby and there was Stormy, my parents, her parents, my cousins, uncles and my son. My grams had him today while I went to church, since I stayed the night with Stormy.

All of them hugged me and my father had the evilest look on his face. He gave me a hug and whispered her days were numbered in my ear. I could fight it and ask them not to bother her but what for? They're gonna do what they want anyway.

"Tha fuck happened!" We all turned around and Haven was standing there with Ariel. All of us gave him a weird stare.

"WHAT?" He barked.

"Did you and Ariel come together?" Armonie asked the question we were waiting to hear the answer to.

"Hell no. She was outside when I got here." He said in a serious tone.

"Hmmm." Armonie had her index finger under her chin.

"That's weird because I didn't get a chance to call her, so how would she know?" Again, all of us waited for him to answer.

"How the fuck am I supposed to know?" He walked over to me and everyone started talking again.

"What happened and Armonie mind your business." He said quietly which let me know they definitely messing around.

Haven is private and after the mess with Juicy, he and I spoke and he was hurt. He also promised himself to never make any other chick his girl. If he is messing with Ariel, he doesn't want anyone to know because if it don't work out, he won't hear the end of it.

"OOOOOOOH BITCH!" She grabbed Ariel's hand and pushed her out the door.

"She so got damn nosy." He said and I started laughing.

"Ariel's a good girl bro." He let a small grin creep across his face.

"Tell me what happened and who I'm about to send the Reaper after?" Colby Jr. and Jax walked over and listened to me tell the story.

"That bitch brought it to the church? She bold as fuck." Colby Jr. said and all three of them gave each other eye contact. I knew too well what it meant.

"Just scare her and her mother. Nothing can happen to her right now."

"A'ight but when the dust settles its lights out." I nodded and all of us headed out the door.

"You ok babe?" Stormy asked when everyone walked out.

"I'm good. Thanks for coming." She wrapped her arms around my neck.

"I'll go anywhere to make sure you're safe." I smiled and kissed her cheek.

"Let's go do some things together."

"You ain't said nothing but a word." She and I stepped out the police station and saw Armonie pointing back and forth to Haven and Ariel. I hope he treats her well because Ariel is not going to allow him to do the things Juicy did.

Armonie

"You walking funny." Colby Jr. said. We were walking to our cars. I tried to get the scoop outta Ariel, but she told me not until we got home. I don't know why she was holding it in when I figured it out.

"Nigga don't talk about the way my daughter walks." My father was very protective of me and so were my two uncles. If you read their story you know why.

"Pops, I'd never refer to the limp. Look at her walk. Somethings different." They all focused their attention on me and I stopped at my car door.

"You got something to tell us?" Colby Jr. asked again with a smirk on his face.

"No and stay out my business." I became very defensive and started my car. I could hear them speaking about me because my window was down.

"She fucking." My uncle Wolf said, and my dad threw his keys at him. My mother stared over at me and I put my head down.

"Nigga she ain't gonna be pure forever."

"Fuck you!" Those two went at it for a few minutes.

"We'll talk later." My mom said and told me to call her when I got home.

Instead of going to my house, I went back to the hotel room. I left VJ there and told him I'd return afterwards. I have to admit, the more sex we had, the more comfortable I became with it. He was always gentle and the one time I asked for it rough, I regretted it. I didn't complain because I asked for it but I won't again unless I'm drunk. It took me two days be ok to walk.

He was supposed to leave yesterday but stayed and he took Mecca back to Virginia weeks ago. The same day, he was here and haven't left except to see his parents, check on the businesses down in VA, or search for a place here with Brayden.

His cousin picked some spots for him and VJ approved but he wanted more than one for options or some shit he said. It didn't make sense, but he told me he had a few houses in Virginia. I thought it was crazy but then again, I share a condo with Ariel and have a whole apartment in the hotel I own. I didn't plan on getting my own house until I had a family. I didn't need all that space right now.

"You staying here now?" I turned and saw Freddy sitting in the lobby. I didn't go through the back because I wanted to speak with the manager. I wish I had though.

"What are you doing here Freddy? I told you we were over." I finally mustered up enough courage to leave him alone. I sent him a message and blocked him from everything.

"I thought we discussed us never being over." The manager looked at me and I told her it was ok for now. I took a seat in the lobby next to Freddy. He was not going in the office to abuse me.

"Freddy we're no good for one another. You have a hand problem and I'm tired of it." He moved closer and grabbed my hand.

"I'm sorry Armonie. I've been going to counseling to work on my anger. You're correct about me not loving you right." I moved his hand off mine.

"Freddy its too late."

"WHAT?" And just like that, he snapped. I nodded my head at the manager to give her the cue.

She's the only one who knew VJ had been staying there with me and how abusive Freddy has been. Its no doubt she's going to get him; especially after he threatened her if she ever forgot to mention this man bothered me. VJ was super overprotective of me now. I don't know if its because of the abuse or me reminding him of his mom.

"You better not be fucking nobody." I rolled my eyes.

"Is that all you're worried about? If I gave my virginity away?"

"Hell fucking yea. You made me wait all this time, so its only right I get it." I couldn't believe he admitted it.

"Too late nigga, I got it and ain't nobody else ever touching her." VJ stood behind him in a t-shirt and basketball shorts. Freddy looked from VJ to me.

"Don't you have a girl and aren't you fucking my sister?" Now it was my turn to stare at him.

"Yea, that's' right. You're the nigga I saw dipping out the house last week." VJ didn't say a word.

"Armonie don't want you here, so I'm giving you a chance to bounce by yourself or with my help."

"Nigga you don't scare me." Freddy was talking tough until VJ snatched him up, took his ass out the back and damn near killed him. VJ beat Freddy so bad he was almost unrecognizable.

I called the cops and had them take Freddy away after filing a complaint about him stalking and trying to assault me. After they left, I went to my room with VJ and the manager in tow.

"Can you give us a minute?" She shook her head and left us alone.

"The only person I'm sleeping with is you and its gonna stay that way." I recited the words he said to me at the party Freddy's mother had.

"Monie, its not the way he's making it seem." He tried to explain but I was so hurt, nothing he was saying made sense.

"Were you at his sister's house with Latifa?"

"Yes but with…" I held my hand up.

"I know the rules of a man who has a side chick so I can't question the things you do. Its not my place and I need to play my position and stay quiet."

"Monie, you and I both know you're more than a side chick to me." I tossed my head back laughing.

"Did you break up with Mecca? Huh?" He remained quiet.

"Do we go out in public and show our relationship off? Have either of us mentioned the other to our parents?" He put his head down.

"I'm afraid you have it wrong then VJ. You may not wanna call it what it is, but the fact remains, I am your side chick."

"Ok, I'm your side nigga."

"Again, in the beginning maybe but you watched me send him a message breaking up with him. You saw me block him from everything. I never answered the phone for unknown numbers which most likely was him. So you became my man even though we never made it official."

"This is bullshit Monie. We were doing fine and he comes spitting bullshit and you won't even let me explain."

"No, its exactly what was supposed to happen. He did what any man would do for a woman he wants. He let me know you were doing you in the process, and how can I be with you and not him?" I started picking his things up and placing them in his duffle bag.

"I don't know why I even agreed to be a side chick knowing you lived states away and you'd be sleeping with other women." He swung my body around.

"Look at me." He had my chin in his hand and used his thumb to wipe away the tears falling.

"Things are fucked up right now but Armonie Banks you are the only woman I've been with."

"He says different and you admitted to being there so it's not much left for us to say." His phone started to ring and both of us looked at it.

"I'm asking you again. Freddy knows about us, have you told her." I folded my arms.

"Exactly! Go home to your woman VJ."

223

"Fuck her Monie."

"Yea its fuck her because she's not here but y'all have history. You live down there with her and lets not forget you been having sex with her even after you broke my virginity. And before you say it, no man has touched me and you know it. Its the reason Freddy is mad." The ringing stopped and started again.

"Thank you for these amazing three and half months, I'll never forget it." He's been here longer but him and I have been together intimately for these last few months.

I left him standing there and ran down the hall. I hid in one of the maintenance closets and heard him yelling my name. I can't even tell you how long I was in there. All I know is I ended up falling asleep.

****

"Are you ok Ms. Banks?" The janitor asked when he saw me on the floor.

When I ran in here, I cried until I couldn't cry any more. I was in love with VJ and its probably because he was my first. We spent a lotta time together, I enjoyed his company and I

224

really thought we were going to be together. Why in the hell I thought that is beyond me? I know what he did to her, he'd do to me.

I guess when you're missing attention at home, you'll welcome it from anywhere. Even if its with another woman's man. This is my karma because I had no business being a side chick.

"I'm ok. I just needed a break. Is anyone in the hallway?" I asked and he turned and told me no.

"Ok. Do me a favor and don't mention to anyone about finding me in there." He smiled and told me never. I walked to my room and the door was slightly opened. I pushed it and saw Ariel sitting on the couch.

"Hey."

"Don't hey me. Why my cousin call asking to find you because he don't know where you went?" I shrugged my shoulders.

"Mmm hmm. Anyway, this was on the table." She handed me an envelope. I opened it and started tearing up.

Armonie, I don't know where you went but I get it. You were right about me allowing you to accept being my side chick. It wasn't fair to you or Mecca and I feel like shit. I've never cheated on her but somehow you coming into my life, had me doing just that. The crazy thing is I didn't look at it as cheating because I wanted it and you. I no longer wanted Mecca and planned on breaking up with her in person. It should've been done before she left Jersey and I apologize for it.

What I won't do is admit to sleeping with Latifa because its not true. Yes, I was there but only because Mycah fucked her. She got tired of hearing me say no and moved on to him. I tried to explain it to you but the tears running down your face and the anger in your voice, told me its best if I leave. I'm leaving from here and I wish you nothing but the best. I will always be your protector if you need me but you have a huge family that can too. I can't reach you in Virginia if he tries something. I'm begging you to tell them. It's the only way I know you'll be safe.

Love always VJ

226

I ripped the letter up and threw it in the trash. I didn't want anything from him and since he's gone, why keep it? He's on his way back to her so I may as well forget about everything we did. It was fun but I have to get back to my life and it starts by me finally telling my family. VJ was right about one thing and that's, that if Freddy comes after me again, he won't be here to save me. If I tell my family, they'll keep me more protected.

Ariel

"The new place is ready. You wanna come see it with me?" Armonie wiped her eyes and shook her head yes.

"Awww bookie come here." I hugged her and she broke down crying harder.

"What's wrong?" She moved away and ran in the bathroom to grab tissue.

"Besides me falling in love with someone else's man, not much."

"Huh? Please don't tell me it's my cousin." I had my fingers on the bridge of my nose.

"Ok. I won't. Let's go." She grabbed her things and left me standing there looking crazy. I glanced down at my phone and saw Haven calling me.

"Yea." I closed the door and walked out slowly. I didn't want Armonie hearing us speak.

We haven't gotten the chance to discuss how me and Haven got together. Everyone knew we were messing around now because of her shouting it at the station but no one knew we damn near stayed together.

"You coming over tonight or am I coming to you?" He asked in the phone causing me to smile.

"Let me call you back later."

"Ariel it's either me and you tonight or I can go to the top four on my list."

"Haven, I don't have time to be dealing with your mother because I stabbed you." He busted out laughing.

"Something happened with Armonie. I'm trying to find out."

"What's wrong with her."

"Boy calm down. She's in love with someone else and it ain't Freddy."

"About damn time. I hope the dude thorough." I wanted to tell him my cousin is thorough, and he knows first hand but until Armonie confirmed her and VJ, I wasn't gonna make assumptions.

"I'm sure he is. I'll call you back."

"A'ight." He hung up and I laughed.

We've been sleeping together for the last few months and the feelings have developed for me but I don't want to tell him. He's not tryna be in a relationship and as far as I know, I'm the only chick he's been with. He's waiting on me after work and makes me stay with him when I'm off.

When he leaves the house, he's usually back within an hour or two and we fucking. If there is someone else, she ain't getting what I am and that's attention, his time and the keys to his place.

I felt a little uncomfortable at first accepting the key because his ex used to be here a lot. Then I remembered we've been around one another for years. I did make him get a new bedroom set because I wasn't sleeping in no other woman's bed. He gave me a hard time but then handed me the money and made me get it.

He is definitely spoiled when it comes to sex with me. Both of us are addicted to the other and to be honest, he's the best I've ever had. If you go by his name, you'd assume he was shitty in bed but it's far from the truth.

"How you in love with VJ when y'all barely around one another?" I asked and started my car. I had to pry.

"It's a long story and right now I just wanna lay down. Can you pull over?" I did and she vomited on the ground.

"What the hell did you eat?"

"I think it's because I'm so upset. You know how I get." I nodded because growing up if Monie stressed herself out too much, she'd throw up. The doctor said she has acid reflux when she worked herself up or some shit.

"VJ is a good guy Monie but he's taken and so are you."

"Not anymore. I broke up with Freddy but you're right. He's taken and I never should've gotten caught up." I handed her a napkin and pulled off.

"Caught up?" I wanted to ask if they had sex because I know like she did, Freddy would flip if he knew someone else took what he's been waiting years for.

"Yea. We'll talk later. I'm getting a headache."

"Ok." I left it alone and drove to the new house I got us. My dad had some being built and let me pick one. He said I needed a home and not a condo.

"Where are we?"

"At our new house." She stared at me.

"House? Ariel you know we were only staying in the condo until we got married. We made a pact to purchase a house when we had a family." She's right. Neither of us wanted to live in a house with no one to share it with. She has money and could purchase her own, but I enjoy having her as my roommate.

"Let me find out you don't like living with me." We started laughing.

"Anyway, what's up with you and Haven and don't tell me my eyes were deceiving me." She asked getting out the car and walking up to the door with me.

"We having fun."

"Fun my ass. You've been staying out a lot and one night, I swore I heard you moaning out his name in the guest room." I covered my mouth.

"I didn't say anything because I was half sleep but now I see it wasn't a dream." She folded her arms.

"Y'all been fucking for a minute."

"Fine! After him and VJ fought, he came by days later and we slept together. He stopped by again and we've been sharing a bed ever since." I unlocked the door.

"Ok now." She glanced around the house from the doorway.

"Am I gonna have some little Reaper cousins soon." She rubbed my stomach.

"Hell to the no. We use condoms and both of us check when we done to make sure it didn't bust."

"Are y'all a couple?" She asked and stepped in with me. I closed the door and we walked around the place.

"No." She stopped and turned around.

"Are you expecting anything from him as far as being a couple?"

"To be honest, I wouldn't mind him being my man but he told me straight up he's not ready to be in a committed relationship."

"Ariel." She had a sad look on her face.

"I know I deserve better."

"You do sis. I love my cousin but he's gonna mess up and you seem like you're feeling him a lot. I don't want you to get hurt like me."

"Like you?" She snickered like a school girl.

"Haven may not be committed to anyone, but he loves sleeping with different women. We both know that. Ariel, you're about to graduate and there's more good men out there who will treat you better."

"Damn Armonie. You sound like me talking to you." We shared a laugh.

"He threatened me already." She stopped.

"I can't be with anyone else and I don't wanna place anyone in danger because he doesn't care."

"So you're in the same situation as me; only he doesn't beat on you and gonna kill you if another man fucks you. Let me find out you threw it on my cousin."

"What can I say?" We gave each other a high five and finished going through the house. I dropped her off at the hotel because she wanted to make sure the room was cleaned. I never did ask about the stuff with my cousin. Oh well, I'll ask tomorrow.

****

"Hey." Haven answered on the first ring. I closed the computer down and focused my attention on the conversation I was about to have.

"Baby, I passed my exam. One more and I'll be a RN." I all but shouted on the phone.

I was now walking outta work and I knew he was at the club because there's a party. He asked me if I was coming but getting off at 11 and going home to get dressed would be too much. I decided to sit this one out and wait for him at his house like always.

"That's good. Real good." He said but something about the way he said it made my antennas go up.

"Where are you? I wanna celebrate and you know how." I hit the alarm on my car and sat down.

"Got dammit." I heard shuffling in the background.

"What's wrong?" It sounded as if he fell.

"My phone dropped. I'll hit you up later." I didn't respond, hung the phone up and pulled off. Haven thinks I'm stupid but let's see if my intuition is correct.

I drove straight to my old condo, took a fast shower, threw on some dressy shit and hauled ass to the club. Armonie and I hired movers to come this weekend and since she's staying at her parents, I didn't want to stay here alone, which is why I've been staying with Haven.

I parked in the back of the club and prayed the side door was open. When I realized it wasn't, I had to save face and go through the front. There was no line because it was after 12 in the morning which meant everyone who was coming is probably already there.

The guy at the front door must've been new because I've never seen him, and he didn't ask if I was looking for Haven like the rest of the security did.

The place was packed and I had to maneuver in and out of people to get by. I stopped when I noticed security at the stairs leading up to Haven's office. I had one of two choices. Take my chances and see if they let me up or yell out somebody has a gun and hope they move. I went with the latter and shit became chaotic. Security stayed put but moved up closer to see what was going on, giving me easy access to go up the stairway.

I prepared myself for what I'm about to see because after hanging up on Haven, I tried calling back a few more times and he didn't answer. Again, I'm no fool so watching this naked woman giving him head shouldn't surprise me. I don't even wanna think about them having sex, which may have already taken place but fuck it.

"Shit girl. Suck all of it out." He moaned with his head back and eyes closed.

"This is why you couldn't answer the phone for me?"

"Oh shit." Haven jumped up and the girl wiped her mouth.

"Haven, I didn't know you had a girl."

"He doesn't. I'm not sure why he stopped you." He sat there staring at me.

"Can you give us a minute?" Haven said continuing to keep his eyes on me.

"Sure. Don't be long because I'm tryna ride that ride again tonight." She grabbed her clothes and stepped out. I'm not even mad at her.

"Drained?" I questioned as he sat there with his dick still out. I closed the door and shook my head.

"You know my father said to leave you alone because you weren't ready. Armonie said you were gonna hurt me but noooo. I had to be hardheaded and continue messing with you." I picked up the Tito's bottle and poured me a drink.

"Do you mind putting your dick away? I don't wanna see her slob all over it." He fixed himself and stood.

"I should've left you alone when I caught feelings because like you said, love don't live here anymore right." I used my index finger to poke where his heart is.

"You told me I was number one in your top five and I laughed it off. There's no way you had a top anything because we were always together." I poured another shot and tossed it back.

"Do you know when I got the results for my exam, you were the first person I called. My parents don't even know yet." I took another shot.

"You seemed happy but then I don't know if you telling me that's good, was meant for me or the BITCH YOU WERE IN HERE FUCKING!"

CRASH! I tossed the bottle against the door.

"I'm a damn good woman Haven and whether you say it or not, I deserve better." The tears started racing down my face.

"Better than a man who can't claim me. A man who has a got damn top five, ten or whatever. A man who cares about no one but himself. And a man who can't even look me in my face knowing he fucked up." He sat in his chair continuing to do other shit and not speak.

"I've never been a woman to act out over a man. I hate who you made me into." I grabbed my purse and stormed towards the door.

"Remember what I said about you being with someone else." Is what he managed to say. I turned and he was now staring at me.

"I don't give a fuck about you being the reaper Haven. I'm going to find me a good man. Someone to treat me better and build with. If you wanna kill me in the process, go ahead. Walking in on the man I fell in love with getting his dick sucked has already killed me inside. Goodbye." I slammed the door, walked to the stairs and went tumbling down.

"Shit. You ok?" One of the security guys helped me up.

"I'm fine. Can you open the side door for me?" He did and it felt like my arm was about to fall off. It had to be broken. He asked if I wanted him to walk me to my car and I declined. Haven would probably murder him for being nice.

I walked alone and unlocked the door. When I checked my arm is was black and blue and already swelling up. I drove down the street and called Armonie. She was half sleep but woke up when I mentioned needing the hospital. I told her where I was and twenty minutes later, she drove me to the ER.

"You want me to stay with you?" She asked when the nurse came in to take me to X-ray.

"No sis. I'm ok. I'll call you when I get home." She hugged me and I told her I'd take an Uber and pick my car up tomorrow. After three hours in the ER, I ended up with a broken arm and dislocate finger.

"What happened to you?" I sucked my teeth at Eddie who was standing there.

"Stop the attitude Ariel. I messed up by promoting those lies but I do care about you." I blew my breath and took a seat on the bench while I waited for the Uber.

"Let me take you home." I rolled my eyes.

"I'm serious. It's the least I can do." He smiled and I laughed. I canceled the Uber and waited for him to pull the car around. He helped me in and off to my condo I went. Haven had the nerve to call me back to back. I shut my phone off. *Fuck him.*

Haven

"Clean this shit up." I told the janitor who was here cleaning up after the club closed. Ariel threw the bottle against the door and glass was everywhere. Usually he came during the day, but he requested tomorrow off, which is really today. He had to take his wife to the hospital for tests.

"Ok sir. I don't want no problems." He put his hands up.

"My bad yo. I'm not mad at you." I said and handed him $100. He tried to give it back three times until I yelled.

"Girl problems." He laughed.

"Something like that." I picked up my drink and took a sip as I stared down on the empty dance floor.

After Ariel left outta here crying, I stayed in my office for the remainder of the night. Marlena tried to come back to fuck again but I told security not to let her up. My head was messed up after seeing Ariel hurting. All the years Juicy and I were together she's never caught me with another woman. Why do the words I hate you hurt when someone says it?

I definitely had strong feelings for Ariel, but I kept pushing them away. I didn't wanna fall hard and she does me the same as me ex. Brayden told me to leave her alone if I was gonna cheat but I couldn't after getting the first taste. It's like we were addicted to one another. Plus, I didn't want anyone else to have her. Of course it's selfish but I never thought I'd get caught. To be honest, we were together so much lately I didn't have time to be with another woman.

Marlena's a stripper and I've fucked her numerous times. The sex is decent and she's been begging for me to dick her down but I never did. Tonight, the drinks were in my system and I couldn't pass up her fat ass. I'll never blame the alcohol because I'm fully aware of where I stick my dick but it doesn't help when you're being tempted.

"You good?" I asked the janitor. When he said yes, I rushed out to go home to shower and change. I needed to speak with Ariel. She was beyond hurt and the least I could do is explain. I admit she had me at a loss for words but I'm good now.

"Boss, how's Ariel?" One of my security dudes asked. I placed my gun on his temple and his hands went up.

"Tha fuck you mean is she ok? You let her upstairs to catch me with Marlena."

"Oh boss, I didn't know that happened. I was asking because she fell down the steps and one of the other guys came to get me." He said with a concerned look.

"What?" I pulled my gun back.

"They said she rolled down the stairs. I tried to walk her to the car and offered to call someone but she refused."

"Was it bad?"

"Her arm swelled up pretty quick and she cried walking to her car."

"FUCK!" I put the gun in my waist.

"Thanks and my bad for pulling the gun out. I'm going through some shit."

"It's all good. I'll make sure to let your sister know when I get home." I laughed because he's my sister's fiancé. They've been together forever, and he's actually cool as hell. I should've known he wouldn't let me get caught but Ariel had my head fucked up.

"Got damn snitch."

"I'll be that. Also, I accept the invitation to take paid days off." He laughed, hit me up with the peace sign and left.

I picked my phone up and called Ariel back to back. She had the audacity to shut her phone off.

I jumped in my car and raced to the hospital. By the time I got there the nurse said she left twenty minutes ago. I didn't waste time going home and decided to stop by her house. On the way out, I noticed Armonie's car but why is she here? If Ariel is gone, I don't know why she hasn't left. I called her phone and she let it go to voicemail each time. I hit Colby Jr up and had him try to reach her.

I parked in front of Ariel's condo and there was a car behind hers. I never seen it and since Armonie's at the hospital, I know she doesn't have company. I stepped out, walked to the door and used my key to get in. I know they're moving but I still had mine.

There was no one in the living room and I could hear noises coming from upstairs. I took the steps two at a time and went straight to her room. It was like de ja vu all over. Clothes were spread out on the floor and the shower was going.

"I told her not to fuck with no one else and here she is showering with the nigga." I spoke to myself as I followed the clothes in the bathroom.

"Shit." I heard her say and my anger went from 0-1000 real quick. I took my gun out, cocked it back, opened the shower curtain and placed the gun on her head.

"You thought I was playing?"

"HAVEN!" Her eyes got big as hell.

"Nah, it's the fucking Reaper."

VJ

"I know he's fucking the bitch from Jersey and if he's not with the dirty one, it's his cousins' friend." Mecca said to her shiesty ass friend Lily. Yup, the same one who tried to fuck.

"But why you mad when you almost fucked Raheem?"

"Sssssh. Bitch be quiet."

"What's the difference if he is fucking someone?" Lily asked and I waited for the answer.

"The difference is I won't ever sleep with another man. I messed up even allowing Raheem to kiss me but when it comes to touching; absolutely not."

"Kissing is touching."

"Are you on my side?" Mecca asked.

"Oh course. I just don't understand if you feel like he stepping out, then do the same." I stood in the doorway of Mecca's bedroom listening to her talk to her friend.

I returned from Jersey a few days ago and today is the first day I stopped by to see Mecca. Between work and tryna figure out if I wanna move to Jersey, she wasn't on my to do list.

Then, I get here and she wanted to have sex. As soon as I said no, she caught an attitude. I ignored it and fell asleep in the room. I woke up to her and Lily's conversation. It didn't matter to me one way or the other at this point if she were with another man because I'm done.

After spending all that time with Armonie, it only verified me being over Mecca and its not because I took her virginity. Monie was smart, held intelligent conversations and had no problem putting me in my place if I made her mad. The thought of another man touching her is something I never wanna envision which is why I spent my days in Jersey with her. I hadn't broken up with Mecca yet, so I understood why she was upset.

I left her the note because I knew she wouldn't speak to me after her dumb ass ex accused me of sleeping with his sister.

The day he's speaking of was a week before he showed up at the hotel. Mycah and I stopped by some chicken place

248

and Latifa was there. She caught an attitude when I told her to beat it. What do you think she did? Yup, went and flirted with Mycah. He's a straight dog and when she offered the pussy, he took it.

We went to her house, they fucked, and I passed out on the couch from drinking with Freddy's pops. Its crazy how Freddy's dad was cool and he was a fuck nigga.

Long story short, I got up the next day and walked out to start the car. Mycah had already came down and told me she was about to give him some head real quick and he'll be right down.

Freddy was coming in from somewhere and smiled when he saw me. I knew for a fact he wasn't with Monie because I spoke to her the night before and she was staying at her parents. She even called me on facetime as he walked in, still at her parent's place. I wish she would've let me explain but she was too upset. I wasn't sure if she told Ariel yet, so I didn't call and ask her to speak to Monie. I did have Ariel check on her though because she ran out and I couldn't find her.

Its all good though because I'm leaving in a few days to go back to check on her.

Vanity and I had a long conversation and she's moving in a couple weeks. I'm gonna wait an extra month or so and then see where my head is.

"What you doing here Lily?" Mecca jumped and turned around while Lily stuck her finger in her mouth like she was sucking a dick behind her back.

"Came by to check on my girl. I'm out." She grabbed her expensive ass purse and left. I shook my head. I thought she would've been kicked out by now but she came up with the rent for the next couple of months.

"Hey baby. You feel better?" I looked at her.

"There's nothing wrong with me." She ran her hands up my chest from behind.

"You don't usually turn down sex, so I thought something was wrong." I turned to her and stared.

"We're finished Mecca." She backed away.

"What?"

"You heard me. This relationship is over."

"Why now? Is it because you found someone in Jersey?" I popped the top off the water bottle and took a sip.

"Why you say that?"

"Because we were on good terms before going there. Now you're ready to break up. Its obviously someone else."

"Actually, I'm not in love with you and never have been."

"Excuse me." She was definitely offended.

"You heard me. I care and have love for you but that dangerous type of love people have for their significant other isn't there for me." Her mouth fell open. I went in the room to get my stuff.

"I thought it would come eventually but the longer we were together, the further away I felt. All the arguing and fighting over stupid shit took a toll on me too. Then, to hear about this Raheem dude is a blow to my face; especially when we hang around the same crowd."

"No, its because of those bitches in Jersey." I shook my head laughing.

"This is what I mean. I'm tryna talk and tell you why its not working and you assume its someone else." I folded my arms.

"And even if it were someone else, you let her slide right in because all you concerned yourself with is tryna keep me on a leash, when you should've been loving me the right way."

"I… I… don't know what to say." She stood there lost.

"Ain't nothing to say." I glanced around her place.

"I don't have anything here that I can see. If you find something, you can toss it." I opened the front door and bounced. I sat in my car and picked the phone up to facetime Monie. It's been a few days so she should've calmed down by now.

"You better be dying if you're calling me." She spoke with an attitude.

"Whatever. Where are you? Its dark as hell out there and its late." It was after midnight and the time zone is the same.

"None of your business."

"Armonie don't play with me." She sucked her teeth and told me at the hospital with Ariel. My cousin fell and she brought her in. Ariel told her she could leave and she did but went back because she felt bad.

"Ok but why you outside?"

"Duh. I was about to get out until this taken man called my phone." She turned her lip up after getting smart. I laughed at her being petty.

"Well this taken man is on the market again." I started my car and placed the phone in the cup holder. She was still on facetime and I'm about to tell her I'll be there soon. We had some making up to do.

"Oh yea? How is that?" I noticed her constantly turning her head.

"I told her I wasn't in love with her. Who are you looking for?" I asked. She was making me nervous and I wasn't even there.

"No one but I feel my car moving; like someone's pushing it."

"WHAT?" My heart started beating fast as hell.

"VJ, I think someone is out here."

"Start your car and pull off." She went to do it and outta nowhere, her car door swung open and her body was yanked out. The phone must've fallen because I couldn't see anything, but I could hear.

"Ahhhhh. Please stop. VJJJJJJJ! Help me. Please stop." I heard and was about to dial 911 on the other line. I couldn't hang up and something else happened.

BOOM! BOOM! Someone knocked on my window. I looked up and it was Mecca. I put my finger up and dialed 911. I had them on the phone and felt like shit because I didn't know the name of the hospital to send the cops. Monie's phone hung up when I clicked over and it infuriated me more because I had no idea what was going on. I called back over and over but it rang and went to voicemail. I sent Brayden a text asking him to go to the hospital.

BOOM! BOOM! I rolled the window down to a crying Mecca.

"What's up?"

"I love you VJ and I'm not about to let another woman have you."

"Go head Mecca. I got other important things to think about." I turned my head when a notification popped up and felt something sharp digging in the top of my shoulder and then my neck. I turned around and this bitch had a fucking pair of scissors in her hand. I grabbed my neck and blood started pouring out.

"Are you crazy?"

"Crazy over you." The bitch jammed the shit so hard in my collarbone, I thought I was gonna die. I opened my car door and started chasing her with the scissors still in me. The bitch was screaming like a maniac.

"Fuck!" I said to myself as dizziness washed over me. I dropped to my knees and hit the pavement head first.

To Be Continued…

CPSIA information can be obtained
at www.ICGtesting.com
Printed in the USA
LVHW090325021019
632927LV00001BA/53/P

9 781090 933232